THE ITALIAN'S
Marriage Bargain

ANNIE
WEST

THE ITALIAN'S MARRIAGE BARGAIN
Book 7, Hot Italian Nights
Copyright © 2018 by Annie West

ISBN: 978-0-6484551-0-3

This is a work of fiction. Names, characters, places and incidents are either the product of the author's imagination or are used fictitiously, and any resemblance to actual persons, living or dead, business establishments, events or locales is entirely coincidental.

Cover Design and Interior Format
© **K**ILLION

Prologue

MASSIMO CONTI SIPPED HIS COFFEE and let his eyes rove the panorama from his hotel balcony. But the picture perfect view of Venice's Grand Canal didn't hold his attention. He had no interest in antique churches and crumbling *palazzi*. He was here for one reason only, and it wasn't the scenery.

He breathed deep, inhaling the scents of fresh-ground coffee and recent rain on old stone.

For years he'd avoided the problem, buried it under the mountain of work required to save his family's ailing business. Driven himself to recoup and transform what his father had almost lost, not just to restore the old man's pride as he slowly recovered his health, but so Massimo's younger siblings could have the future they deserved.

He'd told himself the problem didn't matter anymore. That one day he'd deal with it. Tidy up that single loose end.

Except it was far more than a loose end, wasn't it?

His jaw firmed as he remembered the party

in Milan last week. Valentina's warm, curvaceous body pressing against his side, her hand light on the sleeve of his jacket. The invitation clear in her soft voice and glowing eyes.

Massimo had *wanted* to accept her invitation. Had *wanted* to end the evening in her bed. He'd craved the mindless bliss and the comfort of a woman's body cradling his, slim arms around him, silky skin warm to the touch. Craved it so badly even now he wondered how he'd found the strength to kiss her hand and walk away.

But he had.

Because Valentina wasn't Gina.

The air squeezed from his lungs.

Even after all this time he couldn't move on from *her*. Despite the pain Gina had caused. Despite her fecklessness and her shallow promises that in the cold light of reality meant nothing.

Heat licked his belly as fury and desperation rose. And sexual frustration. Seven years of it.

All because of one woman. One woman who'd promised him the world then spurned him. Who'd torn his heart from his body and kept it. His jaw clenched so hard it ached.

Gina made it impossible for him to find pleasure or solace with any other woman. She'd damned him to a purgatory of torment where he could neither move on nor forget. She drove him crazy.

Because, God help him, he still wanted her. Still needed her.

What sort of fool did that make him?

His gaze flicked to the tiny table where the maid had placed his breakfast tray. To the pages of the newspaper fluttering in the brisk breeze off the canal.

He didn't need to turn to the headline page to recall the text. *Lovers off screen too?* And the picture that took up most of the page. Of Gina Moretti, the glamorous actress, in the arms of her co-star, Matteo De Laurentis. Ostensibly they were here in Venice shooting a film, but the photo showed them on the small balcony of a hotel bedroom, with no camera crew in sight. Their body language was that of lovers.

Massimo grimaced and slammed the tiny cup down. The coffee had turned sour.

Was she having an affair with De Laurentis, despite the fact he was married? The notion curdled Massimo's belly. He had to swallow to keep down bile. The woman he'd known, or thought he'd known, would never consider it.

But then Massimo hadn't known her as well as he'd thought, had he?

He braced himself on the balcony railing, fingers biting into stone.

The hell of it was that, even if it were true, even if she were having an affair with a married man, Massimo still wanted her.

He refused to dwell on what that said about his male pride. He'd spent seven years trying to eradicate her from his heart and it hadn't worked.

He glanced at the newspaper. That article gave him the leverage to ensure he got what he'd come for.

Massimo's mouth turned up in a grim smile.

It was time to get his wife back.

Chapter One

SHE WAS AS GORGEOUS AS ever.

The realisation shouldn't have rocked him but it did. Massimo's pulse slammed to a faltering stop then gathered itself into a sprint that played havoc with his breathing.

In his business Massimo knew exactly how well sympathetic lighting, and where necessary, airbrushing, could hide flaws and enhance appearance. Gina needed neither. She was seated in the full glare of light streaming through the dining room windows of her hotel. The purity of her profile, the soft magnolia of her skin, not to mention the tumble of bright coppery red curls, needed no enhancement.

With a professional eye Massimo took in her dark purple dress with its large poppy print. In the old days Gina had favoured more neutral shades. The pop of strong colour suited her.

He'd avoided, as much as possible, viewing her films or media reports about her since they separated. Seeing her in the flesh, as alluring and vibrant as ever, slammed a fist to his solar plexus.

For a second Massimo was thrown back to the first time he'd seen her. She'd been just twenty-two, eager and nervous about her part in a stage production. He, at twenty-five, with several years' experience in set design, had strolled into the theatre with the cocky self-confidence of youth. Till she'd looked up at him and the world had eclipsed to just one bright, beautiful woman.

He'd looked back later and known he'd begun falling for her then.

They'd been married less than six months later.

Massimo paused in the entrance to the almost-empty room. *Beauty is as beauty does.* Had this particular beauty been playing with another woman's husband? Ice carved a hole right through him, frosting his veins as he remembered that incriminating photo.

Or had the pair, as another article claimed, merely been rehearsing?

It didn't matter. Soon he'd have Gina where he wanted her. She wouldn't have the time, energy or inclination even to look at another man.

~

'Gina.'

She froze, the hairs on her nape and bare arms prickling to attention. The peppermint tea she'd just sipped rose in her throat and she had to swallow hard to keep it down.

The lines of the script she was reading blurred and she blinked, horrified to find that the prickling wasn't confined to her flesh. It was at the back of her eyes too.

Because that voice was the voice of her past. The voice of her faded dreams.

He still had the power to affect her after all this time.

Which was why she'd refused to respond to the invitation she'd received yesterday, no, the *command,* that she meet him at his hotel.

Just knowing Massimo was in Venice too was enough of a shock. But they'd long passed the stage of having anything to discuss. Their relationship had been over so soon after it began.

Slowly she lifted her head. In the process she realised, to her horror, that her hotel's dining room was empty but for them. Even the crew had gone. Filming had almost wrapped up and everyone was eager to get it finished, but she had a late call today.

She was alone with Massimo Conti.

Her husband.

A thrill of...no, not fear, but perhaps trepidation, skated down her spine.

He wanted something and she had a horrible premonition that didn't bode well. She'd barely slept last night, thrown into a state of near-panic after receiving his message. Now, even without looking, she sensed trouble in the air.

Finally, when she could delay no longer, she met his eyes, more grey than green and as sharp as ever under slashing black brows. Instantly her wariness increased. Adrenalin overloaded her bloodstream and she was torn between wanting to scream at him to stop looming over her and wanting to run for her room.

One glance was all it took to realise he was as potently attractive as ever. More so, with an air of almost lazy authority and latent physical power in that tall, lean frame. His dark hair still threatened to flop over his forehead and the line of his mouth was so familiar something wrenched inside her at the sight of it.

How she'd missed him.

No! Not *him*! She'd missed the illusion of what she'd believed him to be. But when the going got tough the real Massimo Conti had been nothing but disappointment and cold, distant disapproval. As selfish in his own way as the father she'd never known, who'd taken what he wanted from her mother then disappeared when she got pregnant.

For a second Gina wondered again how different things might have been if *she'd* got pregnant. But their situation had been fraught enough without a baby.

She ignored the great lump in her throat and raised her eyebrows.

'Massimo. Fancy seeing you here. I thought you were staying on the Grand Canal.' Only the best for the head of the Conti fashion house.

When they'd met and married she hadn't suspected he was the scion of one of Italy's wealthiest families. It had come as a belated shock to discover he was one of the Contis who'd made a fortune manufacturing silks and fabric then clothes and now high-end fashion.

He inclined his head, his expression unreadable. 'I am. But as you refused my invitation I decided to meet you here.'

'It didn't occur to you that I said no because I had no intention of meeting you, there or anywhere?'

Because she was old enough and cautious

enough, now, not to inflict unnecessary pain on herself. Because she'd learned the hard way that Massimo Conti could only bring her disappointment and heartache.

'Why? What have you got to lose?'

Too much. Far, far too much.

Just sitting here, looking up into a face that had once been so dear to her, hurt. The pain wound through her like a ribbon, drawing tight around her vital organs.

But Gina wasn't the heart-on-her-sleeve girl she'd once been. She hid her feelings behind a calm façade, as if her pulse wasn't thudding like a marathon runner's.

'We have nothing to say to each other anymore, Massimo.' As soon as she spoke she regretted it. Because it was the first time she'd said his name aloud in years and something inside, something buried in the darkest, most secret part of her soul, stirred at the sound.

She read the inevitable glint in his eyes. Massimo had never been able to resist a challenge.

That, she guessed now, was one of the reasons he'd begun dating her, the naïve young actress who'd refused the advances of every other single man in the stage production, and a few of the married ones too. No doubt it had been fun parading his success where others had failed.

Without asking, he pulled a chair out from her table and took a seat. One knee brushed hers and she swung her legs away, feeling a rush of sensation up her thigh that slowed to a warm eddy between her legs.

Gina blinked and made a show of closing her

script while all the time she fought panic. One inadvertent touch. Just one, and she was melting.

She needed to get rid of him fast.

'What are you doing in Venice, Massimo?' Her chest felt tight and she had to work to project the words.

'I'm here to see you.'

Gina sat back abruptly, astonished. 'Me?'

Since when had Massimo travelled anywhere to see her? Even when they were ostensibly together, which wasn't long, he'd demanded that she follow *him*, give up her job and probably her whole career, for his convenience.

There was only one possible reason for him to go to so much trouble. He wanted a divorce.

It was long overdue. One of them should have done something about it ages ago, but there had always seemed a reason for not bothering to formalise their separation. Work, travel, the desire not to face the disaster they'd made of their short marriage.

'You have divorce papers you want signed?' She had to call on all her acting skill to keep her voice even.

His hands were empty so he must have them in the inner pocket of his jacket.

'You want a divorce?' His voice was sharp, almost discordant.

'Don't you?' Just because she hadn't pursued one didn't mean she was opposed. It was the logical next step. Yet Gina felt her stomach drop like a heavy rock thrown into water, plummeting so fast it made her nauseous.

'Why?' Massimo planted his hands on the table

and leaned towards her, his jaw set at a decidedly aggressive angle. 'You have another partner in mind? You'd like to legalise a love affair?' Contempt dripped from each word and Gina recoiled.

'You've been reading the press reports about Matteo De Laurentis.'

Massimo folded his arms, the movement drawing attention to the power in his upper body. One sable eyebrow flicked up.

'They're hard to miss.' His tone was even but his expression was disapproving.

With anyone else Gina might have defended herself and said there was nothing between her and Matteo but work and mutual respect. And the fact that Gina had become friends with Matteo's wife Angela, who'd written the screenplay for the film they were making.

Instead she looked straight back into Massimo's brooding dark features and waited. They were long past the stage where she had to explain herself to him.

'Nothing to say?' The tendons in his neck drew tight and his tone was whiplash sharp.

'No.' Gina crossed her arms. 'Nothing.'

She heard a low sound that she couldn't identify. It sounded like...surely he wasn't grinding his teeth?

'Just tell me why you're here, Massimo.'

'It's a private matter. I'd prefer to discuss it somewhere else. Your room perhaps.'

Instantly Gina shook her head. There was no way on earth she'd invite this man into her bedroom.

Even if he did visit her there sometimes in those frustrating dreams that left her wound too tight and aching for a man's touch.

'This is as private as it gets.' She cast a look around the large room. The staff had cleared the other tables and were obviously leaving them alone to chat in peace. As if talking with Massimo could be described as peaceful! Her heart still drummed too fast and she felt flushed and off balance.

'Very well. There's something I want you to do for me.'

Gina stared across at that handsome, determined face and couldn't conjure words to express her outrage.

He wanted her to help him?

'Why?'

His mouth tipped up at one side and a wicked gleam shone in those narrowed eyes. 'Well, you are my wife and you're perfect for what I have in mind.'

Gina's core temperature soared as she imagined what he was thinking of. Except it couldn't be that. Not after all this time. Even though their sex life had been phenomenal. Massimo had proved beyond doubt that he didn't need her anymore, even for her body.

Which was a dismal fact, given that *her* body was blatantly primed for him.

'What did you have in mind?' She crossed her arms, not caring that he'd read her defensiveness.

'I want you to come and live with me in Milan.'

Chapter Two

AFTER YEARS IN THE ENTERTAINMENT
industry Gina was quick with a riposte and
not easily shocked, but Massimo's words stunned
her into silence.

Live with him. In Milan.

She felt the breath shiver out of her mouth, then
the quick, desperate inhale when her brain finally
realised she needed air.

Massimo wanted her to *live* with him?

She studied his features, looking for some soft-
ening, something other than adamantine resolve.
Some hint of attraction, desire, even liking.

There was nothing. Just those shrewd eyes, narrowed on her as if reading every thought.

Her mind was blank with shock. Until the one
emotion she'd forbidden herself to feel unfurled
and blossomed low behind her ribs.

Hope.

In the first year of their separation hope had
kept the pain fresh and alive, for surely the man
she loved would see reason and come to her? As
the years went on and there was no contact from

him at all, much less an attempt to bridge the gulf between them, hope had faded. Yet still it sprang up from time to time, making her miserable when the futility of it hit her. That's when she'd squashed it underfoot once and for all, telling herself her marriage to Massimo was over. Dead. Never to be resurrected.

Now, suddenly, it seemed she was wrong.

'Why?'

His eyes widened a fraction. Had he expected her simply to say yes and pick up where they'd left off years before? She recalled how he'd expected her to obey him without question. From what she'd heard of his growing commercial success, he was probably used to underlings hurrying to do his bidding.

'Because I want you.'

If she'd been stunned before, Gina had no words to describe her feelings now.

For seven years she'd told herself Massimo wasn't good enough for her, even though it was she whom his snobby family, with its wealth and powerful connections, had deemed unworthy. Massimo hadn't stood up for her, hadn't supported her. Hadn't wanted her enough to put their marriage first.

Now he wanted her?

Her brain told her she should be outraged.

Her heart...

Her silly heart performed a dance that left her breathless and wondering. Could it really be? After all this time?

Gina stared across into his cool eyes, searching for some glimmer of warmth. *Needing* it. Because, despite what she'd told herself ever since their sep-aration, life wasn't the same without Massimo. She still craved what they'd had for such a brief time. Still craved him.

'Why?' She didn't trust him.

And there it was. For a split second she glimpsed something in those crystalline depths that spoke of heat and hunger, of desire and raw pain.

In answer her heart leapt so high it seemed to lodge in her throat, blocking any further attempt to speak. Her hands curled around the arms of her chair as she clung on tight, filled with an atavistic fear that if she moved, even breathed, the fantasy would crash to splinters at her feet.

And she was right.

A second later he spoke, making it clear it had been an illusion, that dreadful, wonderful expres-sion in his eyes. An illusion created by her own stupid yearning.

'The House of Conti will be showing its couture range during Fashion Week. As head of the com-pany I'll be hosting some events and I want you at my side, as my hostess for the week.'

Pain crashed through her.

Who'd believe she could have thought, even for a second, that he wanted her for herself? That he burned for her, yearned for her, the way she, fool that she was, had yearned for him?

The illusion shattered all right, so that when she swallowed it felt as if broken shards of razor-sharp glass coated her throat.

But Gina didn't so much as blink as she stared back at him. She didn't permit herself to flinch, even though the pain wasn't confined to her throat. It enveloped her, an echo of the anguish she'd borne for so long after they separated, and which she'd convinced herself she'd grown out of.

Despite the hurt, or perhaps because of it, she found it easy to lift her eyebrows in surprise, and season her voice with just the right amount of mockery.

'And what Massimo Conti wants he gets?'

'Usually.' He didn't even have the decency to look ashamed.

'Not this time.' Gina curled her lips into a smile that conspicuously didn't reach her eyes.

'Oh, I think I will.' He sat back, crossing one long leg over the other, the picture of tailored elegance in his sharp suit and casual shirt. The expression of nonchalance on those long, lean features irked her.

'You'll have to find someone else to act as your hostess. I'm not available.'

'But it's you I want.'

This time Gina was ready for the shaft of longing that carved a ravine through her middle. This was a cruel parody of the loving words he'd once whispered to her. Then he'd claimed to love her. And he'd wanted her for herself, not as some convenient society hostess.

But then he'd proved how much those sentiments meant, hadn't he?

She'd believed they had a love that would last forever. But their forever hadn't lasted long. Now he rubbed salt in old wounds, demanding her presence for an event, a mere week's business!

'Why?' He still hadn't given her a proper answer.

For the first time since he'd arrived, Gina sensed real discomfort in him. His tall frame was too still and the muscles in his jaw were tighter than before.

'Would it be such a bad thing?' He spread his hands in a gesture of openness that was utterly false. He was hiding something. 'Wouldn't it be good for your career to be seen there, and with me?'

If he tried to look modest he failed miserably. There was nothing bashful or modest about those spare features or that self-satisfied air.

'My career is going perfectly well, thank you for your concern.' It was too much to resist adding a sarcastic note. After all, he'd expected her to throw that career away without so much as an explanation, and bury herself in his family's estate. Because she, and her work, were deemed an embarrassment. 'I don't need to be seen with a clothes salesman to get attention.'

Was that quirk of his lips a ghost of a smile? She was sure no-one else would dream of calling the CEO of Italy's newest couture success story anything so prosaic.

'But positive publicity never hurts, does it? Especially since the stories about you lately have been negative.'

Gina stiffened. 'That's none of your concern. Matteo and I can handle that.' Telling the plain truth – that they'd only been rehearsing a scene – hadn't worked, so they'd tried their own diversionary tactics.

Yesterday she and Matteo's wife, Angela, had spent the morning together. They'd visited the Piazza San Marco in the full glare of paparazzi attention solely to prove they were friends, not rivals. Then Matteo and Angela had very publicly spent a romantic afternoon together while she'd gone out with Niccolo Marchesi, the handsome racing driver. So far their damage limitation plan seemed to have worked. Soon the unfounded gossip about her and Matteo would die, when everyone saw how besotted he and his wife were.

Matteo and I.

How easily the words slid off her tongue.

Because they were lovers?

The grinding ache that Massimo had carried since seeing the storm of publicity sharpened to a stiletto blade of jealousy. If Matteo De Laurentis were here he'd rearrange his pretty-boy features for him.

Massimo drew a slow breath and made himself focus. He knew to take media reports with a grain of salt. If the press were to be believed, the women he'd dated and slept with in the last seven years would fill the *Teatro La Fenice*, the famous Venetian opera house, to the brim. It was possible that Gina and De Laurentis weren't lovers. Though he couldn't imagine any man saying no to his stunning wife.

Years ago, when he'd first seen her, she'd looked like a coltish version of a renaissance angel, stepped down from an old fresco. His Gina had been an innocent too, but deliciously, satisfyingly passionate.

He had a sudden, vivid recollection of her, delectably rumpled and sprawled in white sheets, stretching with the sinuous sensuality of a born seductress. Her eyes had shone in invitation, her mouth a pout demanding attention.

Now she was even more beautiful.

And she was *his* wife, damn it. Not De Laurentis's or anyone else's.

Now he was sitting across from her, breathing in that faint scent of vanilla and pear and watching her eyes flash with curiosity, he wondered how he'd managed to go so long without her. Just being in the same room roused his testosterone to dangerous levels. And that gnawing hurt was back again, confirming that this was the one woman he'd ever wanted in his life permanently.

'Staying with me is the perfect way to scotch those rumours.'

She shook her head so vigorously burnished waves bounced around her shoulders. 'Out of the question.'

'You refuse?'

'Of course.' She widened her eyes in haughty surprise. 'It's a ridiculous idea.'

Massimo hid his annoyance, easing further back in his seat and touching his fingertips together. 'That's a shame. The press furore was bad enough when they believed you were sleeping with a married man. What will it be like when they learn you're married too?'

He gave her credit that, but for a widening of her eyes and the sudden fade of her creamy skin to parchment white, Gina gave no reaction.

'Are you trying to *blackmail* me?'

'Blackmail is such an ugly word, don't you think? Persuade is more appropriate.'

For their hasty marriage was still a secret. It hadn't originally been meant to stay that way, but when their relationship turned to ashes there'd been no reason to tell the world and every reason to stay quiet.

A zap of electricity fizzed between them, the air charged by heightened emotions. Those dark blue eyes glittered with a lethal fire.

Curiously, Massimo welcomed her hatred. It was better than the cool disregard she'd shown earlier. As if he meant nothing to her anymore. That had ripped open the chasm of loss within him.

He wanted to *matter* to her.

He'd known, when he came to Venice, that he still needed Gina. His desire for her hadn't died. Nor had the feelings he'd tried to smother with years of work and responsibility.

'Go to hell, Massimo.'

I've already been there.

Time might have eased the anguish to bearable levels, till recently when he'd been unable to think of anything else but the need to fix this untenable situation. But for the first years after their separation, life had been just that, the suffering of the damned.

'In that case, my dear wife, brace yourself for a flurry of the worst possible publicity.' Massimo paused in the act of levering himself from the chair and raised one dark eyebrow. 'What will your precious De Laurentis think of that? He's sunk everything he has into this film, and borrowed heavily from investors. If the public takes against the film's stars and refuses to support it...' He let the sentence hang.

'But at least you won't have to give interviews to the press about our secret marriage.' He raised one hand as if to forestall any comment. 'I'll save you that. I'll speak to them myself. I'm sure I'll be able to provide enough juicy details to satisfy them.'

Blank with shock, Gina felt her stomach swoop like a kite caught in a downdraft, about to smash to earth.

'Why are you doing this?' The words, a husk of sound, were out before she realised.

Massimo had washed his hands of her years ago.

Silvery grey-green eyes fixed on her but there was nothing cool about them this time. His stare burned her skin. She felt flames lick her stomach and breasts.

Surely not! He didn't want her like *that*! Not anymore.

Then his expression altered and she was looking at the urbane businessman, all ease, except for the obstinate thrust of his jaw.

'Let's just say that being together in Milan will be mutually beneficial. You'll be able to put an end to the last rumours of an affair with a married man. I'll get a beautiful hostess whose professional reputation will be a draw for the House of Conti. *After* it's seen you're with me instead of De Laurentis.'

Gina clamped her teeth together rather than give this devil the satisfaction of hearing her rant.

So, after all these years, he'd found a use for the wife he'd forgotten. She, or rather her celebrity, was to be a drawcard for his business!

Her vision misted at the idea of being used in this way. By the man who'd demanded the impossible, then washed his hands of her.

If it weren't so preposterous the irony of it would make her weep. Years ago she hadn't been considered good enough for his fussy family. The impulsive elopement that Gina had thought so romantic had actually been Massimo's attempt to keep their union secret from his relatives. They'd only been together a short time when he'd left her for long months on precious family business, only to turn around and throw in the career he adored, demanding she do the same. Because the top lofty Conti family couldn't cope with a mere performer in their ranks.

'You can—'

He cut across her words before she could finish. 'And if you need another inducement, when this is over, I won't stand in the way of you seeking a divorce.'

The words slammed into her like bullets.

Crazy that in the heat of the moment she'd forgotten the divorce. It's what she'd thought this was all about. That he'd come to get her to sign papers.

Crazy too, that after everything he'd just said, the word divorce should cause those old wounds to bleed anew.

Gina snagged a shaky breath.

'I thought,' he paused and leaned closer, eyes watchful, 'you'd do just about anything for an easy divorce. You want to dissolve the marriage, don't you?'

The blood was rushing in her ears. That's why Massimo suddenly didn't sound quite as certain and self-satisfied.

'Gina?' He sounded almost gentle.

Only because he's negotiating to get what he wants.

Her name and star glamour to back his brand since his company had only just branched out from ready to wear into haute couture. Plus an easy divorce so he could get on with his life. He probably had some aristocratic girlfriend lined up to become the next Signora Conti.

A spasm cramped Gina's abdomen and she had to concentrate on breathing through the pain.

Massimo shouldn't have the power to hurt her anymore. Yet he did. That was the single scariest thing about this whole awful scenario.

He hurt her because she'd never got over him and moved on. He'd been her first, her only love. She still bore the scars of their failed relationship, even after all this time.

That alone was reason enough to act. She had to cut free of Massimo, and the past. She had to make a new life for herself, looking only to the future. Today had proved that she couldn't go on like this.

Gina looked him straight in the eye and made herself smile as if he'd just promised her the moon, no matter how crushed and sore she felt. 'In that case, you have a deal.'

Chapter Three

THREE WEEKS LATER GINA STEPPED inside the apartment that was to be her home for the next week. She sagged back against the door, grateful for the fact Massimo wasn't here and she'd had to use the key he'd sent.

She didn't want to face him yet.

Walking back into her husband's life, even temporarily, was almost more than she could bear. Emotions she'd told herself were long dead had nipped at her heels ever since that meeting in Venice.

Nipped at her heels? More like gouging great chunks out of her insides as the past came alive again to torment her. So many regrets...

Just being with Massimo that day had tested her to the limit. He'd looked so good, even better than the young man she'd fallen for. But beneath the suave countenance and take-charge air of business was a man far colder than she remembered.

How could he even *think* of inviting her to share his home for a week? He'd truly become ruthless. Clearly the memory of their brief period of happi-

ness, and the heart-breaking wrench of separation
meant nothing. Not when there was a buck to be
made out of having Gina Moretti, actress and dar-
ling of the gossip magazines, at his side. To him she
was merely an asset to be used.

Gina shivered and pressed a hand to her roiling
stomach. Her pulse thrummed with nerves as if
she'd just stepped onto a stage on opening night.

In a way she had. For this week she'd play a part.
Publicly she'd be Massimo's escort, hostess for his
parties and, as far as public speculation went, his
latest girlfriend.

Her jaw clenched at the cavalier way he'd manipulated her into playing that role. It was demeaning
and humiliating.

But it was nothing compared with the part she'd
be adopting beyond the public gaze. The part of a
woman who was totally immune to her husband.

Gina sighed and let her head loll back against
the door. She *should* be immune. Her only feelings
should be rage at the way he used her.

But to her shame there was still a kernel of something softer. Something even his callous attitude
and seven years of separation hadn't killed.

Gina hefted an unsteady breath and told herself
she could do this.

She could avoid Massimo when they weren't at
one of his precious events. True, sharing his apartment, there'd be times when they'd bump into
each other. But Gina would be on her guard. It
would be all right.

Straightening, she looked around the entry hall.
Lofty ceilings and long windows gave an air of
spacious charm in keeping with the gracious old

building, which was probably heritage-listed. But the interior was modern, from the gleaming marble floor to the asymmetrical mirror on the facing wall that showed a woman whose face was too pale and whose mouth crimped tight.

Gina shook her head and stood taller. She'd have to do better if she was to play this role.

Grabbing the handle of her big, pull-along suitcase, she crossed the foyer in a deliberate, hip-swaying stroll that projected insouciant confidence.

Now, if she could only convince herself that's how she felt...

Minutes later she was in the guest suite. The space was decorated in shades of grey and gloss white and the furniture was all modern, making Gina recall Massimo's fascination with cutting edge design. Gina's own taste ran to bright, funky and a little retro, and this place should have been too cool for comfort. Yet someone had softened the potentially stark room.

There was a bowl of bright, bronze roses on the bedside table and another on the coffee table where a carafe of hot water and a selection of teas waited for her. Magazines were stacked beside a minimalist chaise longue and a series of paintings along one wall gave colour and warmth. Gina moved closer and saw they were set designs. A series of exquisitely detailed stage sets for a famous opera production.

Gina blinked and felt a rush of memory so strong she had to lock her knees to stand against the force of it. She remembered these. Massimo had discovered them in some bookstore. Hidden treasure, he'd called them. Even though the style of the sets was outmoded by modern standards, they were beautiful. Massimo, of course, had seen past the surface beauty to the practicalities. It had been his field, after all, turning bare spaces into marvellous, imaginary vistas.

Is that why he'd succeeded so well at the helm of The House of Conti? Because he understood that combination of practicality and image?

For the first time it occurred to her that, though he'd abandoned the career he loved, perhaps Massimo's new role gave him some outlet for his talent and passions. It had seemed such a waste when he'd turned his back on the theatre.

But not as much of a waste as their marriage.

Gina yanked her attention away from the images and the memories they evoked. She couldn't afford a trip down memory lane.

Yet, as she dragged her case into the adjoining dressing room, she couldn't suppress a tiny glow of relief that the cold-hearted businessman hadn't totally eradicated the man she'd once loved with all her innocent heart.

That glow faded when she saw the collection of clothes hanging in the vast wardrobe. All in shades of grey, fawn and black, they filled one wall.

Gina stepped closer and saw a note pinned to one of them. Tearing it free she read the typescript.

Choose what you need for the week. The black dress is for tonight's dinner.

Gina touched the shoulder of one full-length dress, noting the discreet black and silver Conti label hand-sewn beneath the neckline. Then a tailored dove-grey jacket. Then a shirt of silk so fragile it felt like she touched a butterfly wing.

Her hand dropped and she stepped back, sur-veying the array of matching shoes, again in black, grey, and fawn. Everything seemed to be her size. How did Massimo even know what it was? He wouldn't remember from all those years ago.

But of course all he'd had to do was contact the wardrobe mistress from the film she'd just finished, explain that Gina was staying with him, and request her details.

Not that Massimo would have done it himself. His secretary would have. Just as he'd got someone else to type the note. He hadn't even bothered to sign it.

What, did you expect a handwritten note from your husband? Maybe a few kisses on it too?

The voice in her head was sharp with rebuke and it shook her out of her distraction. Though it didn't quite kill the momentary yearning for the days when Massimo's notes had been passionate declarations.

A shimmy of regret passed through her. But the past was dead and gone, wasn't it? This was now. A present when Massimo's only interest in her was as a tool to promote his family company.

Her mouth firmed. In Venice Massimo had stip-ulated exactly what he demanded of her and she'd had no choice but to agree.

Seven days living in his home. Attendance at a precise number of events at his side. He'd speci-fied how she was to conduct herself. What she was to say to queries about their relationship. That she wasn't to squirm from his touch, that she was to smile and charm and pretend she didn't object to him wrapping his arm around her in public.

There'd been no mention of a wardrobe, especially a wardrobe that was so not the woman she'd become. She'd given up trying to conform in neutral colours years ago, around the time their marriage ended. Now she dressed for herself in bright, bold colours that made her feel good. Looking at the array of perfect clothes in their perfectly chic, discreet colours made her feel sick.

Could she go back to pretending to be the woman Massimo wanted? Gina told herself it was just a costume, like for any other performance, but this stuck in her craw. This wasn't part of their agreement. Massimo hadn't asked, he'd simply ordered.

Indignation sizzled anew. He'd blackmailed her into being his pawn, giving up a week of her life for him. Wasn't that enough? She was a person, not a doll to be dressed to his satisfaction. She'd agreed to be here under sufferance. That was enough.

Massimo would have to take her as she was.

Gina laughed, the sound brittle. Years ago she hadn't been good enough. Now even when he wanted to profit from her celebrity, he tried to stage-manage her into an image that suited him, or more precisely, his family brand.

Beneath the ancient hurt, her resolve hardened. She mightn't be good enough for the Contis but she was happy with who she was.

If that wasn't enough for him, too bad.

Massimo was in the large salon, taking a call,

when footsteps approached from the bedroom wing.

Anticipation burred his nerves. He'd come home to find the apartment silent and Gina locked away in the guest suite. He'd thought about knocking on the door, inviting her to join him in a pre-dinner drink, but clearly she was waiting till the last moment to make an appearance.

Impatience had twisted his gut. But he'd mastered it. Let her take her time tonight. He had all week. Longer. One way or another she wouldn't be leaving. He'd make sure of that.

The eagerness with which she'd finally accepted this deal, her smile when he'd talked of dissolving their marriage, still rankled, sharpening every possessive instinct.

Yet he'd been sure he glimpsed something behind her determined expression. Something that shadowed her glorious eyes. Perhaps her feelings for him weren't as dead as she pretended. Instinct told him she still cared, or if not cared, she hadn't managed to excise him from her emotions as completely as she pretended. He could work with that.

The footsteps stopped and he turned to the doorway.

Massimo's mouth dried and his PA's voice became a drone of sound in his ear. He forced the air out of cramped lungs as a shock wave smacked him full force. He told his PA he'd deal with the issue tomorrow and ended the call.

'You know how to make an entrance.'

Perfectly arched eyebrows lifted a fraction but Gina said nothing. She knew exactly the impression she made in that royal-blue dress that matched her eyes. It didn't cling tight to her magnificent figure. It didn't need to. A scattering of miniscule beads winked with every breath she took so ripples of light fanned down from her breasts to her hips in an enticing rhythm. The hem ended above her knees, and her legs looked endless.

Massimo swallowed, feeling abruptly as if his tie turned into a garrotte. His throat dried as he recalled those smooth, ivory-toned legs tangled with his. The triangle of bright auburn hair at her sex. And her husky, breathless cries of wonder as she gave him her virginity and he gave her first multiple orgasm.

The memory was so vivid it might have been yesterday. He *wanted* it to be just yesterday. Or today.

How had he let seven years pass? It was too easy to say that at first there'd been sheer panic at the enormity of what he faced, then wounded pride when she walked away and didn't look back. He had his old man's stubbornness, so he'd been sure she'd come back and when she didn't, well, he'd had no intention of letting her see how much that hurt. So he'd buried his feelings till he finally realised that was no solution.

He *had* to resolve this.

Heat burned the back of his neck, his palms and his groin. His flesh steamed as he struggled to yank his gaze back up to her face.

There was a knowing glint in her eyes. Damn it. She knew what she did to him.

But he could use that to his advantage. Instead of looking away Massimo let his carnal thoughts show in a smile that bared his teeth. 'You look good enough to eat, Gina. One slow bite at a time.'

There it was. Almost hidden by her sudden hissed intake of breath. A flash of heat in those fine eyes that spoke of arousal.

It didn't last. The next second her expression was scornful. Massimo had what he wanted – for now. Proof that desire was mutual.

'You shouldn't—'

'Of course I shouldn't. My apologies. My mind's on eating. Clearly I shouldn't have skipped lunch.'

A tiny line appeared on her brow as if she wasn't sure if he were serious.

Oh, he was serious all right. Serious about getting Gina exactly where he wanted her. And keeping her.

Chapter Four

GINA STARED AT THE MAN before her. In
formal clothes he looked imposing and dra-
matically handsome. Her foolish heart gave a silly
little quiver of excitement.

She'd told herself over and over that the reason
she'd ensured they never met in seven years was
because she hated him. The dreadful truth was that,
though she couldn't forgive him for the shabby
way he'd treated her, she was still connected. More
than connected. Attracted.

It was there in her runaway pulse, the hollow
sensation down low in her body and the way her
perfectly comfortable dress now scratched her skin,
particularly her breasts, as if she'd suddenly become
hyper-responsive to touch.

At least it was *her* dress that suddenly chafed.
Designed especially for her by Angela's sister. It was
a sign of how far Gina had come that she could
afford to commission a dress for herself. Massimo probably thought it puerile of her to reject
the Conti dresses, but Gina refused to be bought.
That's how it would feel if she put on one of those

elegant, sombre-toned outfits. Not herself, but a woman pretending to be someone more accept-able.

'I didn't come here to be insulted or treated like some inanimate...' She struggled to find an appro-priate word.

'No. You came to help me out.' Massimo smiled again. To her surprise it wasn't a carnivorous grin that transfixed her trembling body with the idea he might sink those white teeth into her neck. It was the surprisingly sweet smile she'd once told herself he reserved for her alone.

No doubt he'd used it on a lot of women since they parted.

'Only because you threatened me into it.' She stood straighter, wishing her heels were higher as he approached and she had to tilt her chin to meet his eyes. 'And because it means we can end this...' Unaccountably her throat closed and she had to pause. 'Once and for all.'

'This *marriage*.' His deep voice drew the word out.

Massimo was just a step away now. Gina caught the subtlest hint of fresh pine-scented soap on male skin. The heat still suffusing her body drilled down through her abdomen to that aching hollow between her legs.

She blinked and told herself she didn't do instant arousal anymore. Not for anyone. It was just that they shared a history. At some level her body rec-ognised his. But once this week was over there'd be no need for them to meet again.

And you think that will make the yearning any less?

'I don't appreciate being manipulated.' It was

better to hang onto anger than allow that pang of regret over their failed marriage. It was too late to save their doomed relationship and there was no sense torturing herself over what might have been.

Yeah. Good luck with that. You've been so successful in putting it behind you. You've never even tried to find someone else who could make you happy.

Gina wished the sniping voice in her head would shut up. Especially when Massimo's shrewd eyes locked on hers. She felt the air escape from her lungs as from a pierced balloon. Her traitorous knees shook till she forced them to steady.

'And for the record, I'm perfectly capable of dressing myself for the time I'm here. I don't need your charity. I may not be as wealthy as the Contis but I make a good living.'

'Ah. That scraped your pride, did it?' Something ignited in those pale eyes. His nostrils flared and suddenly he didn't look like the sophisticated businessman the world saw. He looked like a hunter, focused on his prey. 'You should try having your spouse walk out on you. That really hurts.'

Gina boggled up at him, her mouth opening then closing as she registered that he'd actually accused *her* of desertion.

'Success has obviously gone to your head, Massimo. It's impaired your memory. You were the one who left me. I offered to go with you originally but you wouldn't let me.'

Was it shallow of her to feel a flash of triumph when his mouth tightened? Too bad. She was in no mood to let him rewrite history.

'It would have made things complicated.' He drew a slow breath as if reining in his temper. 'But then later when I asked you to join me you refused. You just walked away.'

Powerful emotion throbbed in Massimo's voice. Curiously it made her insides squeeze tight.

Gina's hands slid to her hips. 'You didn't ask, you demanded. You just expected me to throw in my career for you.'

'And obviously your career was more important than our marriage.'

'What were you offering in return, Massimo?' Her head thrust towards him as her ire rose. 'A role as a downtrodden little spouse, living under the thumb of her in-laws in their tomb of a house? You couldn't wait to get away from it when you were young but suddenly you wanted us both to live there. To give up the careers we loved for the privilege.' She sucked in a ragged breath, stunned at how the old hurt crammed back, filling every crevice of her being. 'And I was supposed to do that even though they looked down on me. They thought I wasn't good enough for you.'

The pain was a writhing beast inside her now, like a dragon, breathing fire that ignited old hurts.

'You're exaggerating, Gina. They—'

'Exaggerating!' She feared she'd self-combust as outrage spiked. She breathed deep, telling herself that all she was doing was hurting herself, and showing Massimo how much he'd hurt her. 'Perhaps you're right. After all, you didn't tell them about me, not even after we were married. How could they look down on me when they didn't even know I existed? Till the day I rang and asked to speak with you.'

Unfortunately that memory was as vivid as ever.

She'd been missing Massimo and worried about the increasing gaps between his phone calls. One day she hadn't been able to reach him even to leave a message so she'd looked up the number for the Conti villa. The woman who answered had been dismissive when Gina asked to be put through to Massimo. Until Gina had told her she was his wife.

But instead of calling him to the phone the woman had screeched at her. Gina hadn't caught every word but two things she'd registered. That the woman's son, Massimo, wasn't married and that she didn't appreciate prank calls.

'I explained that.'

'So you did.'

Massimo had skirted around the truth but it was simple enough. His family had expectations of him. They thought he should marry someone they already knew. Someone from their elite circle. His father in particular had plans for Massimo and as he hadn't been well it was best not to stress the old man too much.

In other words, the future they had in mind for their eldest son didn't include marrying a penniless, illegitimate actress who didn't even know her father because he'd disappeared before she was born. Far from being from the highest echelons of society, Gina was working class and only half Italian. The other half was Scottish or perhaps Irish. Her mother's English wasn't good and the short affair that got her pregnant had obviously not been spent talking.

'Listen, I—'

'Is that the time?' Gina made a show of checking Massimo's designer watch. She trembled at the high-octane cocktail of emotions swirling through her. This had to stop *now*. The past was a dead end. It would get them nowhere. 'Shouldn't we be leaving? We're already late. I thought tonight was something important.'

It seemed Massimo agreed. His eyes flicked to his watch then back to her, impaling her with that grey-green stare that should have been cool but which scorched her right to the soles of her feet. His mouth compressed as if forcing down an argument. The he took her elbow, shepherding her silently towards the door.

Gina wanted to yank her arm free of his hard grasp. It set up a riot of jittery sensation right through her body, reminding her of how she used to respond to Massimo when she was young and naïve. When she thought he loved her and love could conquer all.

Worse still, she realised it was disappointment she felt. Disappointment that tonight's event for the glitterati of the fashion industry was more important to Massimo than them – Gina and Massimo.

See. She was doing it again. There was no them.

Gina breathed deep and pinned on the serene expression she saved for red carpet events and tricky interviews.

One thing was for sure. This unwanted week with her ex was the perfect way to kill those last, sentimental feelings she had for Massimo Conti. When this was over she'd be cured once and for all.

Massimo held himself stiffly as, hours later, he

opened the door and watched Gina walk back into the apartment ahead of him. There was a subtle sway to her hips as she moved, a grace that drew his gaze and made him want to gnash his teeth. His temper and his frustration were at dangerous levels.

All evening he'd watched Gina practise her feminine wiles, charming everyone. She'd laughed and listened, delighted and mesmerised. Even the women seemed to like her, despite her vivacious beauty, for she had a warm, natural manner and showed an interest in others.

And as for the men...

Pain radiated through his jaw and Massimo realised he was grinding his molars. Ahead of him, Gina sauntered towards the bedroom wing as if he'd already been dismissed. The fire he'd been tamping down all evening sparked into flames.

'We need to talk.' The words emerged abruptly but Massimo was past playing a polite fiction.

'I'm tired.' She didn't turn but he saw her shoulders rise.

'This won't take long.'

She swung around, her glorious hair bouncing around her almost-bare shoulders, her eyes wary. For an instant he thought he read vulnerability in that beautiful face. Were those shadows haunting her eyes? Then the illusion disintegrated. She lifted her eyebrows in a show of boredom.

Massimo crossed the space between them in a moment. Gina's eyes widened slightly as she lifted her chin to hold his gaze but she didn't retreat.

Of course not. Gina wasn't the sort to back down. He'd always loved that about her. Tonight, teetering on a knife edge between desire and wrath, racked by jealousy, it was the last straw.

No, the last straw had been when he'd found her posing for photos, arm in arm with Matteo De Laurentis, looking like she belonged in his embrace. Gina had laughed up at the actor, apparently bewitched by his charm and totally oblivious to her husband, caught up in conversation mere metres away.

De Laurentis had noticed though. Massimo had seen the gleam of understanding in the other man's eyes. He'd been about to hustle the star off somewhere private to warn him off ever touching Gina again, when a microphone had been thrust in front of Massimo and he'd been asked about what this season meant for the House of Conti. He'd drawn on acting skills that rivalled anything De Laurentis could muster to appear cool, collected and confident.

All the while his instinct had urged him to do something primitive and violent. Like shove the actor out of the way with a solid punch to his too-handsome face, then sweep Gina up in his arms and bring her home.

Because she was *his* woman. His *wife*! He didn't want other men leering at her, fantasizing about having her.

Whatever had been between De Laurentis and Gina ended now.

Gina shifted, putting her weight on one leg and putting a hand on her outthrust hip. Her stance was combative and sexy as hell, drawing attention to her sultry curves and long legs. 'What's the matter, Massimo? Are you still annoyed that I didn't wear the dress you ordered me to put on?'

Actually, he was. His pride had been piqued by her refusal to wear his present.

'It wasn't an order. It was a request.' When she merely lifted her eyebrows again in a sceptical look, Massimo's frustration boiled over. 'Is it really too much to expect you to wear a beautiful dress, made for you, simply because it has the Conti name on the label?'

The thought she hated him so much made something inside him shrink hard. His gut cramped and he told himself it was with anger, not hurt.

Her mouth tightened and he had the impression she bit back a response. Then, suddenly, words tumbled out in a rush. 'I'm not some mindless mannequin. You and your family thought I wasn't good enough for the Conti name before. Do you really think I'd be comfortable pretending I am now?' Her other hand jammed onto her hip as she glared up at him. 'I might have more PR value now that I'm well known but I'm the same woman I always was. And I make no apologies for that. No matter what your family thinks.'

Massimo rocked back on his feet.

'The dress has nothing to do with trying to make you into someone else.' He was still getting his head around the idea Gina believed he'd ever considered her not good enough.

He felt like the floor had lifted and whacked him in the head.

'As for my family, they're delighted you're here this week.' It was true that, years before, they'd been shocked by his marriage. And, yes, his father had been dead against it. But Massimo had made it clear he wouldn't countenance any disrespect to his wife. Their acceptance of her was the price of him staying to salvage the family business.

But in the end that hadn't mattered because Gina had deserted him. His gut hollowed at the memory of those bleak days, his utter disbelief that the woman he loved had turned her back on him.

'Are they really?' Suspicion glinted in those dark blue eyes. 'Only because they think I'm good publicity.'

Massimo opened his mouth to disagree. His mother, in particular, had been thrilled at the news he'd spend this week with his wife. Clearly she harboured hopes of a reconciliation. As Massimo had before tonight. But revealing that to Gina now...

He drew a deep breath, beating down the urge to forget words and simply act. 'The clothes were a gift. It made sense to give you a wardrobe of Conti clothes since we're spending this week promoting the brand.' He paused, watching her process his words.

'I thought you'd appreciate some guidance on what to wear tonight. As far as I know you've never attended any Fashion Week functions. But there's no question of trying to change you into someone else. As for not being good enough, that's nonsense. If I thought that I'd never have married you.'

Gina didn't respond. She didn't even seem to breathe. Tension thickened the air between them until it became hard to breathe.

She looked up at him as if she'd never seen him before. 'You expect me to believe that?'

Massimo's hands fisted at his sides. All night she'd tested his patience. Now she doubted his word? 'Why wouldn't you? Have I ever lied to you?'

Her stare was so intense it should have stripped the flesh from his bones. But he met her gaze openly, sustained by disbelief and anger. Did she really think so poorly of him?

Gina had always had the power to turn him upside down. But this latest revelation put a different slant on her desertion. He felt like he'd opened a Pandora's box of unexpected secrets and emotions.

'How could you dare to think I was that shallow?' He bit out the words.

She blinked and he caught something fleeting in that obdurate gaze. 'So if you're not upset about the dress, what did you want to talk about?'

It took Massimo a few seconds to yank his brain back to the beginning of their conversation. If Gina thought changing the subject would get her off the hook she was in for a surprise. Bad enough that she considered him a liar. Reminding him of De Laurentis was a dire mistake.

Red hot pincers dug into his belly as he recalled his wife in another man's arms. Not for a movie this time, but because she wanted to be there.

'De Laurentis.' The name was bitter on his tongue. 'You were all over him like honey on bread.'

The earlier paparazzi photos had been bad enough. But with a photo he could pretend it was some other woman, not Gina, snuggled up to Italy's favourite movie star. Tonight there'd been no room to hide from the sight of his wife pressed up against another man, smiling and simpering as if she'd never been happier.

While she looked at Massimo as if he'd crawled out from under a rock.

The sight of the pair had eaten at him like acid through metal. Making him feel like part of him had been chewed away.

Gina stiffened, raising her chin and projecting such an air of hauteur it was a wonder ice didn't crack when she spoke. 'All I did was stand beside him and smile.'

And let him pull her close, his hand on her waist while he murmured something that made her light up from within. Her eyes had shone as they hadn't shone for Massimo in years. The sight of her obvious pleasure in the arms of another man had stolen Massimo's breath. For precious seconds it felt like the world stopped, and his heart with it.

'It was publicity for the film. You understand publicity, Massimo. It's the only reason you wanted me here.'

Not the only reason.

If only it were.

And if only he could believe there was nothing between his wife and Italy's favourite leading man.

Life would be so much simpler.

'You're here in Milan with me. I won't have you embracing other men. Especially Matteo De Laurentis. Understood?'

He strode forward, invading her space, backing her up against the doorjamb.

'I understand all right. You think because you forced me to come here that you can make me dance to your tune, like a puppeteer with some doll on a string.'

Gina's face was flushed and vibrant, full of passion, a passion Massimo had told himself he didn't miss. But it was a lie. He'd missed her for seven long years. Craved her. Even now when she made a fool of him in public, playing up to another man.

'All you care about is your precious company and I—'

Massimo refused to listen to any more. Words weren't working. Nor was control or patience.

He closed his hands around her bare shoulders and yanked her to him, hearing Gina's huff of surprise, feeling it as a puff of warmth against the underside of his chin.

Then, before she had time to protest, he did what he'd wanted to all night. And three weeks ago when he'd seen her in Venice. And every day of every year they'd been apart.

He smashed his mouth down on hers and kissed her with all the ruthless passion that years of rage and loss had created.

Chapter Five

GINA HAD SEEN IT COMING.

She'd seen the feral light in his eyes. Read the brutal intent in that hard body.

Had she twisted away?

Had she ducked her head?

Had she tried to placate him?

She told herself she'd done none of those because she had every right to her anger. Because it was time someone stood up to Massimo and brought him to book when he rode roughshod over them.

But as his mouth plastered over hers, his tongue sweeping past her lips in a forceful invasion that demanded everything, Gina knew the truth.

She'd goaded him. Deliberately.

She hadn't been able to stand there, toe to toe with this man who drove her crazy in the worst and best of ways. She hadn't had the strength to walk away.

Because she wanted this. Wanted him.

Want? Is that what you called this driving force that hammered with every pounding pulse beat?

Want was too weak a word.

Need engulfed her. It was marrow-deep. It was in every pore of every centimetre of her flesh.

She'd needed Massimo for years and she'd just given up denying it.

His tongue probed her mouth, demanding and at the same time challenging her to respond. His kiss was pure carnal invitation.

He pushed her up against the doorway so she was pinioned between it and Massimo's hot, sculpted body. Gina went into meltdown. It wasn't simply that she'd had no lover since him. She hadn't wanted one. Because Massimo had always been the one she wanted, even when she hated him for making her feel that way.

For a moment Gina hovered on the brink of self-pitying tears. It was cruel that the only man she'd ever loved was so bad for her. The only logical response was to break away. Despite his imposing size and his ire he wouldn't force her. He'd have to let her go.

But Gina hadn't cried in years, she wasn't about to start now. Nor would she pull away.

For she couldn't. She simply couldn't.

Not when being in Massimo's embrace felt like coming home.

Through his fine suit Gina felt the outline of bone and muscle, the solid thighs, the jut of ribs, the press of that powerful chest. His heart throbbed a staccato rhythm against her. She tried to tell herself Massimo was motivated only by anger, not real desire. But already the big hands running up and down her bare arms gentled, confounding her.

He tilted his head, searching for the best angle to seduce her mouth. And he found it. Massimo had always kissed like a fallen angel, one who'd mastered both torment and bliss.

Bliss coursed through her now as she tangled her tongue against his, lifting her chin and responding in kind.

A rough sound of approval vibrated from his mouth to hers, from his chest to hers. It sent pleasure spearing to her womb, her breasts, the place inside her elbows where his thumbs brushed, making her shiver.

Gina's hands rose to his arms, fingers digging into fine fabric and taut muscle. She needed more. Their kiss was no longer a demand but a seesawing dance of give and take.

It shouldn't be possible to get closer to him but she tried, rising on her toes and planting her hands on his shoulders to bring her nearer his height.

Massimo's response was to slide one arm around her waist and haul her up till her feet left the floor. She heard a shoe drop as she snaked her arms over his shoulders and clamped her fingers into the thick, dark hair at the back of his skull. Her lips welded to his as rapture beckoned.

He tasted better than the finest wines, better than fresh-picked strawberries still warm from the sun. He tasted like every dream of happiness she'd ever known, and then some.

And when he shifted against her, thrusting a thigh between her legs so she balanced astride it, Gina's urgency took on a new dimension. One that matched his, given the unmistakeable arousal pushing against her.

Her dress rode higher as she squirmed closer, excited by the sensation of Massimo's clothes against her bare skin.

'Gina.' It sounded like a plea or perhaps a vow. But Massimo's broad hand on her leg, pushing the silky material up her thigh was as earthy as it got. She shivered as his baritone growl scraped her soul and those hard fingers curled around tender flesh.

She wanted this, wanted him so badly. How had she gone so long without his touch? Only by freezing her emotions and her needs under a blanket of ice. By living a cold, half-life these last few years.

Gina had forgotten how feminine he made her feel. Feminine and sexy and powerful, despite the shivers turning her body to putty in his hold. Turning her into a woman who'd give her all to this man.

As if sensing her capitulation, Massimo broke the kiss, lifting his head to stare down at her with eyes that glowed with silvery fire. The air was thick with the sound of their gasps and the rapid thrum of her pulse in her ears.

'*Mio dolce amore.*' It was what he'd called her when they'd been in love. When Gina had believed nothing would ever break them apart. Then he smiled. That rare, beautiful smile of welcome she'd always thought Massimo reserved just for her. Because he loved her.

Her throat shut convulsively, almost choking her.

Massimo didn't love her. He was *using* her.

So if that smile wasn't a look of love it was just part of his arsenal of seductive weapons.

Gina hadn't thought it possible to hurt more than she'd hurt before. Yet now, realising even that fragile, falling-in-love period they'd shared had been nothing of the sort, at least for Massimo, she felt sick to the core.

How many women had he used that smile on? How many had he seduced with his superior technique?

Those big hands had pushed her skirt all the way up to the lace of her underwear and his smile was taut with anticipation.

Anticipation that she'd allow him to take her up against the wall, as easily as some street-walker with a promise of ready cash.

Bile rose in Gina's throat. She slid her hands to those broad shoulders and shoved with all her might.

Surprise must have weakened him for he actually stepped back a fraction, allowing her to wriggle off his leg and back down to the floor. The place between her thighs hummed with the demand for sexual satisfaction but it was nothing to the nausea filling her.

'Gina, are you all right?'

'Don't say a word. Please.'

She had no idea what he saw on her face but Massimo took another step away, a heavy frown settling on that long, lean face. Gina swept her bare foot around the floor, searching for her dropped shoe, then gave up. She needed to get away. Now.

Gina kicked off her other shoe and turned, stumbling to the corridor. Massimo was so close she expected to feel his hand on her shoulder or catching her wrist. But he didn't reach for her, just let her scurry, all thought of pride forgotten, to the safety of her bedroom.

It wasn't till she'd snicked the lock shut behind her and sagged back against the door that she

understood what had made Massimo look so worried. There was a mirror on the wall beside the
door and as she turned she caught sight of herself.

Her hair was a mare's nest, tousled and messy.

Her skin was too pale and her mouth was swollen and red.

Her eyes were wide and blank.

But it was her cheeks that really gave her away.
Down each one ran a wet track where the tears
she'd refused to shed for seven years ran without
ceasing.

Chapter Six

MASSIMO PACED THE LENGTH OF the salon, impatience and regret warring within. Last night he hadn't gone after Gina. The sight of her crumpled mouth and tear-stained cheeks had wrenched his gut in two but he'd known she needed space.

From him.

He wasn't a guy who liked emotional scenes. Who was? Yet, to his surprise, letting her walk away was one of the hardest things he'd ever done. Instinct had urged him to follow her, fold her close in his arms and force the issue of their dormant marriage.

Fortunately reason had won out. They'd spent seven years apart. There was too much hurt and distrust between them to be overcome by simply holding her and demanding she give him what he wanted.

Even though he wanted so badly it was an ache through every bone in his body.

What he needed was a plan. Getting her here, in his home, was the first vital step. But he needed far more if he was to smash down the walls Gina had barricaded around herself.

This morning, when he'd knocked on her door at breakfast time it was to find her suite empty and a note in the kitchen saying she'd gone out for an early coffee.

Massimo had glared at the gleaming coffee maker on the benchtop. Gina was avoiding him.

He'd stayed in the apartment as long as he could, till his conscience, spurred by three frantic phone calls from staff, forced him out the door. He'd brought the Conti brand to Fashion Week and he had to ensure it succeeded.

But through the day's whirl of activities, his mind kept turning back to Gina. He'd found an excuse to slip home in the late afternoon, hoping to catch her, but the apartment was empty.

His feelings for his wife had spun over the years from love to outrage, hurt, frustration, grief and, always, desire. Lately he'd faced the truth that she was still part of his life. That he wanted her back.

He'd told himself he'd find a way to make it work.

He hadn't counted on causing her anguish.

Or on his reaction to the sight of her distress.

It had undone him as nothing had. Not even the burden his family had unwittingly placed on him all those years ago. Nor even the emptiness that had swollen inside him as he and Gina went their separate ways. Most of that had been done at a distance. He at the family villa in Lombardy and she out of the country, filming.

He'd never seen Gina in tears. Never seen such terrible pain on her face.

That fact slammed into him like a race car under a chequered flag.

It made him physically ill, remembering.

Because he'd kissed her?

Because she couldn't bear his touch?

Fire licked his skin even as his bones turned to ice. The notion was unbearable.

But then he recalled the avid way she'd clung to him. That kiss hadn't been just about him. Gina had made demands of her own.

Then why was she so upset?

Because that kiss made her unfaithful to her lover, De Laurentis?

Massimo's stride faltered and he came to an abrupt halt in front of the marble fireplace. He grabbed the carved mantelpiece with one hand, sucking in oxygen till the stars circling his vision vanished.

When the security buzzer sounded he thought at first it was the dull throb of pain in his skull. Till it sounded again. Instantly he was across the room, striding into the entry hall and pressing the control panel. Maybe it was Gina. Maybe she'd forgotten her key.

'Hello, Gina?' Massimo didn't know the woman's voice. All he knew in that first instant was the crash of disappointment that it wasn't her.

He closed his eyes and breathed deep, marshalling his control. He wasn't a weak man. He didn't let emotion master him, ever. But in this moment Massimo felt pinioned by despair so sharp it pierced his lungs, winding him.

'Hello? Gina?' The woman's voice came again.

Massimo pressed the button to allow her entry

then waited for her to come upstairs, curious to see his wife's visitor. He opened the door as she raised her hand to knock.

'Oh. Sorry.' She looked flushed and surprised, her blonde hair bright against her dark winter coat. Then recognition hit. Of course he'd seen her before. Angela De Laurentis. Screenwriter and wife of Matteo De Laurentis, Gina's co-star. The man the world believed she'd been having an affair with.

'Signora De Laurentis.' Massimo inclined his head and stood aside with a gesture of invitation. 'Please come in.'

Curiosity and excitement outstripped every other emotion. With luck now he'd get to the bottom of Gina's relationship with her co-star.

The woman smiled. 'You're Massimo Conti, aren't you? I'm so pleased to meet you.'

She crossed the threshold and followed his gesture towards the main salon. That's when he noticed the bulky package she carried.

'Please, call me Massimo.' He gestured to the package. 'May I?'

The woman paused when she saw the sitting room was empty. 'This is for Gina. I haven't missed her, have I?'

So his absent wife had arranged to meet this woman at a time when she thought Massimo would be working.

'She had to go out but I'm expecting her any time.' He'd make sure he stayed till she arrived. 'Please, won't you take a seat?'

Angela nodded and headed for a long lounge.

'Can I take your parcel?' He was intrigued by the fact the two women, who according to the pop-ular press, were rivals for the same man, were on friendly terms. And by the parcel Angela carried so carefully.

She shook her head, placing it gently on the seat beside her. 'If you don't mind, I'd like to give it to her myself.'

Intrigued, he nodded. 'Can I get you something to drink? Coffee? Or,' he recalled that she was half Australian, 'tea?'

'No, thank you, I...' She paused and shrugged. 'Perhaps some water?'

'Of course.' Massimo smiled and watched her relax back against the sofa. 'I'll just be a moment.'

A few minutes later she took the glass he proffered and gave a tentative smile as he sat opposite her. 'I really am glad to meet you.'

Massimo tilted his head in silent encouragement. 'I feel the same. I'm fascinated by the film project Gina's been working on.' Especially her relationship with this woman's husband. 'I hear the screenplay is fantastic.'

The blonde blushed. 'It seems to have worked well.' She paused and looked him directly in the eye. 'You and Gina must be very...close. In Venice she didn't mention having someone special...'

'Yet here we are, together.' Massimo stuck on a smile that hid his chagrin at the fact he'd had to threaten his spouse into sharing his apartment. And a pang of something like hurt that he wasn't significant in her life anymore.

He intended to change that.

'I'm glad.' Another pause then Angela continued in a rush. 'Gina deserves some happiness. I'm so pleased she's finding it now, with you.'

'You like her very much, don't you?' Massimo was intrigued. Many women would feel intimidated by Gina's vivacious beauty and talent, yet he sensed Angela was a genuine friend.

'Absolutely. You're very lucky to have her. I hope you know that.'

Massimo read the warning in her expression. Was she threatening him? The idea intrigued.

'I do.' Even though the relationship, such as it was, wasn't at all as Angela thought. Even though it frustrated the hell out of him right now.

'She helped me through a very rocky time.' Angela spread her hands. 'Then all the world thought she was having an affair with my husband, which was nonsense, as you know.' She rolled her eyes. 'Honestly, the muck they can rake on the basis of a misinterpreted photo! Gina helped me dampen the awful rumours. She even spent time with our friend, Niccolo Marchesi, pretending they were a couple, just to get the paparazzi away.'

Massimo found himself leaning back in his seat, his heart hammering as relief filtered through him, easing tense muscles one at a time.

Here was the confirmation he'd needed. The thought of Gina with De Laurentis had driven him crazy with jealousy. Then he'd seen pictures of her out with Italy's playboy race driver and it had been the last straw. He'd almost scotched his plan to force Gina here to Milan. Except he'd known that he couldn't simply walk away from her. Seven years of separation had proved that.

'So it was all a lie?'

'Of course.' Angela raised her eyebrows. 'Gina's a good friend. One of the kindest, wisest women I know. She understands what it is to be alone and unsure of yourself.' Another pause, as if she selected her words carefully. 'She doesn't talk about her past much but I know she's been badly hurt. Let down by someone she trusted. A *man*.' Angela shot him a meaningful glance that definitely held a warning. 'She's still...bruised from that and I'd hate to see her hurt again.'

Massimo stared back, thoughts and emotions tumbling over each other so fast he felt winded.

Gina alone and unsure of herself.

She had such a vibrant personality he'd never thought of her in those terms. She always seemed so confident. On the other hand he knew she was an only child whose mother lived on the other side of the world, married now to an American and totally absorbed in her new life.

Seven years ago Massimo had felt alone, burdened by family demands he'd felt wary of sharing with his new bride. His father's illness, the shocking revelation that the family company teetered on the brink of failure and the shameful reason for it. Plus the sheer neediness of his mother who'd broken under the pressure.

Gina had seemed so independent, so together, he'd forgotten she'd had no-one but him.

An unseen blade carved a slice through his conscience. Had he been so wrapped up in his family's problems, so ready to take things at face value because of his pride, that he'd missed what should have been obvious?

Gina hurt.

Gina let down by someone significant in her life.

The cynical, disillusioned self he'd listened to

for years said it must have been some other lover who'd broken her heart.

But another part of him felt, with a certainty so strong it was like a thunderclap on a cloudless, sunny day, that the hurt Gina nursed dated from their marriage. *From him.*

Could it be?

He was torn between wanting it to be true and hating the idea.

Gina didn't seem wounded. But then nor did he, to the outside eye.

What about the defiant way she'd challenged him to think the worst, not deigning to explain her relationship with De Laurentis? Or the fiery emotion he'd read in her eyes even when she stared up at him with that chilly look of disdain? Was that because he meant nothing to her anymore, or because she kept secrets like he did?

His hands dug into the soft leather of his chair.

'Massimo?'

He blinked and refocused on the blonde woman before him, realising he'd been so lost in thought that he'd forgotten her. He opened his mouth to say something when they heard the sound of the front door opening.

Massimo was on his feet in a second, turned towards the entry foyer and the woman stepping inside, already shedding her long coat.

She hadn't seen him and he had a moment's leisure to observe the grace of her movements, the lovely curve of her calves beneath the straight black skirt and the even more delicious curve of her breasts against the turquoise of her silk shirt as she turned to hang up her coat.

His response was like a winter avalanche, catapulting through his body, battering down defences he'd spent seven years erecting.

He wanted this woman.

No, he *needed* her.

Last night's kiss had shattered any final pretence that he didn't. Desperation clawed at him. He had to close the distance between them, to make her his. Especially since that kiss had proved she wasn't immune. He'd told himself it would be enough, to begin with, to rekindle the physical passion between them. Yet even as he'd said it, he'd known he wanted far more.

Now, after listening to Angela, Massimo felt a glimmer of hope that perhaps Gina felt more than just the physical hunger which had always been so flammable between them.

Maybe her heart wasn't as closed as she pretended.

Which meant he had to work out a way to get through to her. To break the ice crystals that had formed around her heart. To make things right again.

'Gina.' His voice sounded curiously husky, sharp on the last syllable, making her freeze where she stood, arm outstretched to the coat rack. Massimo modulated his tone to a smoother note. 'You're just in time. I've been having a delightful chat with your friend, Angela. But I know it's you she wants to see.'

There. Just for a second something slipped across his wife's frozen features. Fear?

But she'd only be afraid if she thought Angela might reveal something she didn't want Massimo to know.

Satisfaction curled deep inside.

So it *was* true.

Gina guarded secrets close to her heart. Past hurts. And maybe hopes too?

The idea that Gina might feel even a little of what he did buoyed Massimo. It seemed he'd trudged through a lifetime of darkness and here was light ahead. He grinned and watched Gina's eyes widen as if dazed.

'I'll leave you two ladies alone, shall I? I'm sure you have a lot to discuss.' He walked over to Angela, took her hand and kissed it. 'It was an absolute pleasure to meet you, Angela. I look forward to doing so again.'

The blonde smiled up at him. 'So do I, Massimo.'

He turned, approaching Gina who stood now beside another long lounge. She stiffened as he drew near. He could almost feel the tension twanging through her taut frame.

'Until later, *tesoro*.'

Chapter Seven

GINA CLOSED THE DOOR BEHIND her friend and repressed a shiver.

Until later.

Massimo's words, in that deep voice with the velvety undertone, held a promise she couldn't ignore.

Did he mean to finish what he'd begun last night?

Her skin flushed with heat then cold as she recalled her unbridled responses. Massimo had awoken the girl she'd been seven years before, the gullible innocent who'd given her all to the handsome, charming man who'd introduced her to pleasure beyond her wildest imaginings. Who'd made her believe in happiness.

The whole time she'd sat, chatting with Angela, Gina had been aware of the jittery tingle of anticipation down her spine and the searing liquid heat between her thighs. One heavy-lidded look from Massimo's glittering eyes, one casual promise in that rumbling low voice and she was turned on.

Despite knowing he was no good for her.

Despite her determination not to respond.

Last night she'd barely even tried to resist Massimo's practised seduction.

Pain cramped her belly. How many women had there been since they separated? Massimo could seduce the birds from the trees and sane women into madness. Look at her, believing love could conquer all when her own childhood was proof that lust, not love, ruled and that men couldn't be trusted to stay the course.

No, that wasn't true. Matteo and Angela had had their problems but it was obvious they loved each other deeply. They shared more than physical desire. Love did exist.

That was Gina's problem. She'd truly loved while to Massimo she'd been a passing attraction. A novelty.

'I like your friend.' Massimo's voice was warm, rippling like a balmy wave across sensitive nerves.

Gina's shoulders hitched up, the skin of her nape drawing tight and prickly. Slowly she turned to find Massimo on the other side of the sitting room. He'd shed his jacket and tie and undone the top few buttons of his shirt, giving her a tantalising glimpse of bronzed flesh.

She bit her bottom lip to stop a breathless gasp of excitement. But she couldn't stop that melting sensation pooling between her legs. Because he looked better than ever. Because she'd spent all night imagining what would have happened if she hadn't retreated to her room.

Because, despite the ruthless way he'd manipulated her, Massimo Conti still had the power to seduce her to the edge of insanity. The compulsion to close the distance between them and beg him to seduce her was almost overwhelming. Though it would be easier simply to seduce him. He'd always been breath-takingly ready for sex.

'What do you want, Massimo?' She crossed her arms, furious with her wayward self. 'Shouldn't you be working? With the runway show coming up I thought you'd be busy.'

He shrugged and she wished he hadn't. In his shirt sleeves, with the cuffs rolled up to reveal sinewy forearms, the movement accentuated his powerful frame beneath the fine tailoring. Massimo was tall and lean rather than chunky and gym-pumped, but he was all hard-packed muscle.

Dismayed, Gina registered another ripple of response low inside.

'You're right. I need to go again soon.' Yet he made no move to leave. His stillness, and the predatory watchfulness of that bright gaze, unnerved her.

As did the way she wanted to run her hands over that powerful body and let the carnal appetites she'd squashed for so long have their head. Seven years was a long time, yet not one man had tempted her. Until her husband stormed back into her life.

She gritted her jaw. She refused to think about it, despite the fact her body was a riot of sparking awareness.

'Well, don't let me delay you.' Unwillingly she moved back into the room, heading for the parcel Angela had delivered. The dress made for Gina by Angela's designer sister, currently visiting from Australia.

Gina had admired the stunning outfits Sonia had made for Angela and begged her help. If she had to spend a week pretending to be her ex's partner, she'd do it in style. Her *own* style, not something vetted and approved by condescending eyes in the House of Conti.

'Do I make you nervous?'

Strange. Gina could almost believe that was regret in his tone.

'Of course not.' She'd die before she revealed that. She didn't trust his power over her because she didn't trust herself, especially after last night.

'Then why won't you look at me?'

Gina stilled, clutching the bulky package in both arms. Slowly she swung around to meet his laser stare. She felt it like ice burning her chilled flesh. But far worse was the memory of his supple, clever hands on that same flesh, evoking heat and ecstasy.

'We're not in public now, Massimo.' She swallowed, hating the way her throat closed convulsively on the once-familiar name. Hating how just saying it conjured memories of her whispering his name in the dead of night, hoarse with pleasure. Or laughing so hard at some shared joke that she could barely form the syllables. In those days they'd shared so much. 'We don't have to pretend for an audience.'

He took a step nearer and lifted his hands, palm up. 'Does it all have to be for an audience?'

What game was this? 'I don't want to be here. You know that. I came because you forced my hand. Don't expect me to pretend to enjoy your company when we're not playing your precious masquerade.' Ostentatiously she glanced at her watch. 'I don't have to perform that particular role again for a while.'

He didn't flinch or frown but his mouth tightened. Was he annoyed? Good!

Gina spun away, heading towards her bedroom.

'Gina. Please.'

Her footsteps stuttered to a stop, her heart beating high and hard against her breastbone.

Please?

It wasn't just the word. It was the way Massimo said it, as if it was wrung from his very soul.

She shut her eyes, telling herself not to be sucked in by lies. Or by her own yearning. He wanted something more from her, that's all. Something he'd forgotten to specify when he'd proposed this devil's deal. Maybe he wanted her to suck up to someone important at their next party.

'Gina?'

She drew a deep breath and opened her eyes, taking a second to compose her features before turning towards him.

'What is it?'

He gave nothing away, except for the slight hollow in one cheek as he clenched his jaw.

'There's something I want to talk with you about. Why don't you take a seat?'

Gina was shaking her head before he finished speaking. 'No. Whatever you have to say, just say it. I've got things to do.'

Like telling herself all the reasons being with Massimo Conti was a bad idea. Because the way he looked at her, at once earnest and determined, reminded her of that summer long ago when he'd declared his love and she'd been so swept away by excitement she hadn't paused to question how likely that was after such a short time. She'd fallen for him in a heartbeat, but the chance of him truly loving her? Only an innocent would have taken his words at face value.

His eyes locked on hers as he stepped closer. Not near enough to touch, but at this distance she was fascinated to see his eyes gleamed more green than grey.

'Angela said you'd been hurt by someone. A man.' He drew a slow breath, as if waiting for her to reply.

She couldn't. Her tongue was stuck to the roof of her mouth. Angela had said *that*? Gina wished the honey-toned floor would open up and let her disappear. She'd shared barely a hint of her past with her friend. She hadn't expected her to blab that to Massimo of all people.

Gina jutted her chin higher, her eyebrows lifting, silently daring Massimo to continue.

'It made me wonder if that person was me. If it was *our* breakup that made you so—'

'It doesn't matter.' The words gushed out. 'Angela doesn't know what she's talking about.'

'She seemed to.' Still Massimo didn't look away. All his attention was focused on her, reminding her of the absolute absorption he brought to bear on things that were important to him. But she hadn't been one of those things for many years.

'If that's all I—'

'Because if I hurt you, I'm sorry. I was young and stupid and sure I had all the answers. I know now that I didn't.'

Gina felt her jaw sag. Massimo apologising? It was too much to take in. She was torn between wanting to hear more and knowing it was too little, too late. If he'd bothered to say sorry all those years ago maybe they'd have had a chance. But not now.

Yet instead of changing the subject, of walking away, Gina found herself canting towards him.

'What do you mean – *if* you hurt me? Of course you hurt me!'

He'd said he wanted her but then, as soon as his family called, everything they'd planned, everything they'd hoped for, was suddenly unimportant. She'd applauded his family loyalty but what about loyalty to his wife? Surely there'd been room for compromise, but Massimo hadn't seen it that way. He'd demanded, not asked or explained, much less listened.

'Don't worry, Massimo. I got over it.'

'So you're saying the way you are isn't because of me?'

'The way I am?' Gina drew herself taller, reminding herself she was an expert at hiding pain and self-doubt. He couldn't possibly know how hard this was for her. Yet her mouth dried.

Once more that shrug that made a show of all those delectable muscles.

'You're vibrant, talented and determined, Gina. But there's a brittleness too, as if you don't want me to see how much you feel. You never used to be like that.'

Shock washed through her like a tide, leaving her lost for words. Gina told herself Massimo couldn't possibly tell how she felt. He was guessing, based on her friend's well-meant but unguarded words.

Yet she felt part of her defences crumble as Massimo took another step towards her.

'Stop right there.' She put an arm out, palm facing him. 'Whatever you're imagining, don't. I don't need anything from you, Massimo. Not your apologies or your speculation.'

He stood, scrutinising her as closely as any director watching a day's film rushes.

'I told myself it was some other man who hurt you. Some lover after me. But you know what?' His mouth curled up in a smile that held no humour. 'The idea of you with anyone else makes me sick here.' He slammed a hand to his flat belly, the action reinforcing the stunning impact of his words.

Gina's head spun. Shock vied with anger and, to her horror, delight, at his jealousy.

No. No. No. She wasn't going there.

'You have no right to feel jealous. You gave that up years ago. My relationships are none of your business.'

Even though there hadn't been any relationships. She'd thrown herself into work, telling herself one day, when the time was right, she'd find a man worthy of her love. But the time had never been right, just as it had never been right for her to initiate a divorce. She'd supposed she'd get around to it one day. Meanwhile she wasn't ready for the press frenzy if their spur of the moment marriage became public just because they ended it.

Gina had thought it so wonderful when she left Italy for that important audition that Massimo had followed her, producing legal papers for a marriage. Their whirlwind wedding had been impossibly romantic.

No wonder it had failed. Marry in haste, repent at leisure.

Massimo folded his arms across his chest, the

image of pure, belligerent male. Gina told herself she despised him. Unfortunately she got a secret thrill, watching him.

'We're still married, Gina.'

'Sure. And I suppose you'll tell me you haven't been with another woman since we split.'

As if!

Massimo simply held her gaze with the confidence of a man who knew exactly where he stood, while she swayed like a sapling in a breeze. This conversation was so unreal she still couldn't believe it.

'I am.'

'Sorry?'

'I *am* telling you that. I haven't slept with another woman in seven years.'

Gina slapped her free hand on her hip and huffed her indignation. 'Quit being pedantic. You may not have slept with any but—'

'I haven't had sex since you left me. Is that clear enough?'

Stunned, Gina felt her mouth work but no sound emerged. Shock scrabbled at her windpipe, stopping the breath in her lungs.

'You can't ask me to believe...'

'Whatever you think of me, Gina, I've never lied to you.' His eyes seared her. She was burning up, combusting from the inside out.

'So you've been celibate all this time?' She'd intended to sneer the words but instead sounded merely stunned.

'Celibate and very, very frustrated.'

The blaze of heat in Massimo's steady gaze extinguished any belief that he lied.

Suddenly everything Gina thought she knew about him, about them, folded in on itself, like a box squashed flat. She stared up into the face of a man who looked stripped bare, except for raw honesty and a pride that dared her not to believe him. As if he'd relish the chance to parry her words.

Gina's fingers dug into the soft parcel. Her peripheral vision dimmed and for a second she wondered if she might faint.

But there was no easy escape from this conversation.

'Aren't you going to ask me why?'

She didn't want to know. It was none of her business. Their marriage was over.

'Why?' Her voice cracked on the word.

'Because I never stopped wanting you, Gina.'

Her breath locked and so did her knees, as her legs turned to rubber. Deep inside emotion swirled faster and faster, into a roiling, uncontrollable mass. She felt her eyes widen.

'I *still* want you.'

Gina prided herself on facing what life threw her way, no matter how difficult. Yet, for the second time in twenty-four hours, she wanted to stumble to the sanctuary of her room.

Instead she made herself stand tall, as if he hadn't poleaxed her with his words. As if she didn't fight the urge to snuggle up to him and admit he wasn't the only one wanting. It was just sex. It had to be. She refused to let it be anything more than that.

'Then I suggest you get over it. Because I'm not, *ever*, going to be yours again.'

Chapter Eight

THE APPLAUSE WAS THUNDEROUS, ENOUGH to make Massimo's head spin, especially since he was already lightheaded from lack of sleep.

Roberto, the House of Conti's designer, stood, smiling and nodding, surrounded by models dressed in the stunning outfits that would hopefully take the Conti name to the next level. Judging by the reception from the crowd, some of the richest, best-dressed people across several continents, plus a slew of fashion writers, they were off to a good start.

Years of hard work were bearing fruit. The Conti name was no longer in danger of being dragged through the mire. Instead it shone brighter each day.

Yet it wasn't enough. Work success and family obligations weren't enough. He wanted more. Living in the same space as Gina these last few days had only brought home to him how much he'd missed her, how incomplete his life felt.

'They want you.' The soft voice in his ear was

barely audible over the applause.

He turned as Gina nudged his elbow. He looked down and saw her beautiful indigo eyes held something he hadn't seen in a long time. Pride. Encouragement. Pleasure.

The sight transfixed him.

He'd forced her to Milan with threats. Nothing between them was resolved. Yesterday she'd roundly rejected him and had avoided him ever since, not difficult given his crazy work demands.

Yet here she was, moved by the success of the show. *His* show. Warmth filled him. Because she was happy for his success.

Or maybe she's just showing what a spectacular actress she really is. She's probably relieved to be halfway through this week together.

Urgency cramped his innards. He needed more, so much more.

'They want you up there, Massimo. Go and take your bow.'

He didn't want to leave Gina. Massimo felt good with her at his side. Even if her attentiveness was a charade for public consumption.

But Gina was pushing him forward and the spotlight was on him, so he nodded and went up to accept the accolades. He waved to the crowd as he crossed the room, but inside he felt galvanised with a grim determination. He had to break through to his wife before their week ran out. Nothing, not even the admission he'd been faithful to her, had moved her.

She was an ice queen, cool and remote. Yet he knew, none better, that at heart she was passionate and vibrant. His belly turned molten as he remembered Gina in his arms, feisty and feminine, demanding and delicious.

It had been so impossibly long that just thinking about her response to him turned his walk stiff as he fought to control his body's unruly arousal.

Finally Massimo made it to the podium, acknowledging the applause. This was another huge step towards the success he'd envisaged for the company and it was a real pleasure to give a short speech acknowledging the hard work of the Conti team.

Even so, much of his attention was on the red-headed beauty in a bright fuchsia pink dress that stood out from all the predictable black. She was the most eye-catching, stunning woman in the room. He didn't even care that he'd had to field questions on why she wasn't wearing the Conti label. All he cared about was breaking through to her. Keeping her.

But how could he win her back?

He'd apologised for hurting her. He'd even laid himself bare, admitting he hadn't been with a woman since her. Yet she remained resolutely unimpressed.

He snared her eyes across the crowd and the instant arc of sizzling connection gave him his answer.

It was time for something stronger, something he knew she'd respond to.

Seduction.

Gina hurried into the apartment building beside

Massimo, trying to keep up with his long-legged
stride. She was hampered by eye-wateringly high
heels, but she'd been determined to hold her own
amongst a who's who of the fashion industry,
knowing she'd be under microscopic scrutiny.

The show had been enormously successful and,
despite her seesawing emotions, Gina couldn't
help but be proud of what Massimo and his team
had achieved. The House of Conti would be on
everyone's lips with those fabulous designs. There'd
been a younger vibe to the collection, appealing to
a much broader audience than she'd expected from
an old, family-run company.

Her conversations with Sonia, the independent
Australian designer, had given her a new apprecia-
tion of how much work had gone into reinventing
the Conti label. Especially when Sonia had heard
rumours that Gina hadn't, about some unspecified
but significant problems in the business that had
now been overcome.

What were they? For years Gina had assured herself she wasn't the least bit interested in the Conti
company. Now she wished she'd kept her ear to
the ground.

Was it crazy to respect what Massimo had
achieved? After all it had been at the cost of their
marriage, since he'd demanded she quit her career
to support him while he ran the family company.
How perverse was that?

Gina slanted a sideways glance at the handsome
man beside her and felt that too-familiar tug of
awareness through her insides. What she needed
was distance.

She tried to conjure indignation at Massimo's

outrageous blackmail. But for once that didn't work. Indignation wasn't effective against the man who'd admitted he'd made mistakes in their relationship and actually apologised.

The man who'd looked at her with that sizzle in his eyes and told her he hadn't been with a woman since they split.

Gina told herself it was a tactic to blindside her. But Massimo had never outright lied to her before.

When he'd looked her in the eye and said he still wanted her, it felt like he was about to eat her all up. And she'd quivered in anticipation! She'd only just managed to escape to her room before she did something mind-numbingly crazy like tell him she'd been celibate too, because no man had ever made her feel the way he did.

Crazy indeed! She'd loved him madly but losing him had almost destroyed her. Only stubborn pride and the frantic need to throw herself into acting had saved her.

Gina blinked and realised she'd stopped behind Massimo as he worked the security device on the apartment's front door. She had no memory of coming up from ground level. She'd been so lost in abstraction, thinking about the man before her. The man whose broad shoulders filled her vision and who turned a sombre suit into the hottest thing she'd seen in years.

Gina swallowed hard as he swung the door open and gestured for her to precede him inside.

The scent of spice and pines and hot man filled her nostrils as she hurried past, transporting her to the weekends they'd once spent in the mountains. They'd stayed in a snug little chalet with spectac-

ular alpine scenery that had fascinated city-bred
Gina. Not that she'd got to explore the mountains
very much. She'd been too busy exploring Massimo's toned, hard body with its fascinating ridges
and lines of muscle and its incredible capacity for
pleasure.

Heat drenched her as surely as if she'd walked
into a sauna. She felt her cheeks flame and was
grateful for the painstaking effort she'd put into
her makeup. Massimo could have no idea how he
affected her.

Except, as she looked up to where he now
loomed beside her, it was to find his gaze locked
on the fluttery pulse in her throat. Worse, she'd
lifted her hand to that unsteady throb, so her fingers hovered there, a dead giveaway.

Gina dropped her hand and stepped further into
the apartment.

Massimo moved with her, his tall frame mirror-
ing hers, making her falter to a stop halfway across
the entry hall.

Her heart beat rough and hard and she had to
work to unlock seized vocal chords.

'I need to go and get out of these shoes.' Her
voice sounded scratchy. She forced a smile. 'Con-
gratulations again on your huge success. You must
be pleased.'

'Thank you. I am.'

Yet Massimo didn't look as if he had the House
of Conti on his mind. His gaze traced a line of
fire from Gina's throat, down to the straight cut of
her bodice across her breasts. Too tight now that
her breasts swelled under his regard. The perfectly
comfortable bra she wore now seemed too small

and the silky fabric rasped her nipples like sand-paper.

Gina breathed slowly, searching for control. She wasn't a naïve innocent anymore to be distracted by a man's stare. Even if that stare was glazed hot with arousal.

Even if that stare found its echo in her own eager regard.

She shifted back a half step and once more Massimo mirrored the movement.

'Stop it!'

'Sorry?' His gaze trawled back up, this time to her mouth, and Gina felt a shudder of animal response. Just to his stare!

It was infuriating and unacceptable. It made a mockery of her vaunted independence from this man, this...blackmailer.

'Stop these games, Massimo. I don't know what you think you're up to but I don't want to play. I'd appreciate it if you'd get out of my way.'

Somehow he'd got between her and the door into the rest of the apartment. Gina put a hand behind her and found she'd backed up to a wall.

'I'm not playing games, Gina.' His eyes lifted and she felt herself falling into that mesmerising gaze. 'I've never been more serious in my life.'

Serious about what?

No, she didn't want to go there. She knew that look, just as she knew the once-experienced-never-forgotten tug of carnal excitement low in her body.

'I'm not in the mood for celebrating your success with sex.'

A muscle jerked in his jaw and those brilliant

eyes snared her again. Did she imagine it or was that a splinter of hurt she saw there?

Impossible. Despite what Massimo had said about not being with another woman in years, it was Gina who'd been hurt when they split, not him. She'd left a vital part of herself behind with him, and it had been a struggle to go on, whereas he hadn't once looked back, until he decided he wanted to cash in on her fame.

His mouth lifted at one corner in an expression that revealed grim humour.

'This isn't about celebrating, Gina. This is about us.'

She shook her head, soft curls bouncing around her shoulders. 'There is no us.'

'Are you sure?' His words were whispered but she heard them clearly for now the space between them had dissolved and they stood toe to toe. Gina's head tilted back so she could maintain eye contact. Even in heels she couldn't match his height.

Out of nowhere misery swamped her. That had been her problem. She'd never been Massimo's match, even though she'd wanted to believe he'd be happy with a woman who didn't have a posh family or a fantastic education or a coterie of sophisticated friends.

'Oh, I'm sure, Massimo.' She swallowed and it felt like her throat was lined with ground glass. 'We're over. Over and done with.'

He shook his head, his eyes never leaving hers. 'Then how do you explain this?' One hand cupped her cheek and the other slid around her waist, jerking her up against him and Gina felt, for one precious moment, that she'd come home.

Chapter Nine

IT WAS AN ILLUSION. MASSIMO wasn't her home anymore. This was simply her body's craving for intimacy.

But, oh, the gentle brush of his fingers, the curl of steel-hard muscles encircling her waist, and the furnace-hot solidity of his torso against her yielding body... Even through their clothes he felt appallingly good.

Better than good. Wonderful.

She'd longed for this. And since their kiss the longing had become a craving in her blood, singing in her ears, whispering in the brush of her clothes against over-sensitised flesh.

A bubble of emotion welled high in her throat, clogging her chest as his eyes held hers. Massimo's long fingers danced a gentle, provocative cadence along her jaw then up to the soft flesh beneath her ear.

Gina struggled to repress a luxurious shudder as everything inside her sparked and tingled.

'No. I don't want this.' She sucked in air to fill lungs that seemed to have collapsed. 'I don't want you.'

Slowly Massimo shook his head. 'For a world class actress you're not very convincing. You'll have to do better.'

He was right. Her voice was breathy and uneven and her nipples thrust, hard and puckered, against him. Gina realised she'd actually arched her back in response to the arm wrapped around her waist, tugging her close.

'You want me, Gina. We both know it.'

'No! You're living in the past. I've moved on.' She wouldn't let herself desire him. She had more control than that.

He cocked a sleek, dark eyebrow. 'To De Laurentis?' He shook his head. 'Not from what I hear and I've got a very good source.'

Angela. It had to have been Angela who'd filled him in on that detail. Gina didn't know whether to be annoyed or relieved. It shouldn't matter what Massimo thought of her, yet to her surprise it did.

'And don't try to tell me you've taken up with Niccolo Marchesi instead. I know that was an act to convince the paparazzi you weren't breaking up the De Laurentis marriage.'

Gina stiffened. Angela had been busy. But why had her friend confided so much to Massimo? Angela didn't know he was Gina's husband. As far as she, and everyone, knew, Gina and Massimo hadn't been together long.

Massimo's big hand, sliding from her throat to her shoulder and down her side, jumbled her thought processes.

'Let me go, Massimo.' She stiffened as his palm skimmed her waist then moved down to her hip.

'Trying to force an unwilling woman isn't your style.'

Instantly he stopped. A second later his hands dropped away as he stepped back, leaving her reeling at his abrupt withdrawal.

His eyes narrowed on her flushed cheeks and she felt the pulse at her throat hammer with shock.

It was her opportunity to escape. Except, tragically, she didn't want to. No matter what common sense or pride dictated.

She should give him a glare and step sideways to stride confidently off to the bedroom wing. Even hunching her shoulder against him and scurrying away would do. Instead Gina's feet stayed glued to the floor, her fingers flexed with the need to touch him. Worse, she swayed towards him like iron to a magnet.

Strangely he didn't crow his triumph. His expression was tense, his features severe.

'This isn't a contest or a game, Gina. I want you. I always have. And I believe you want me too.'

She swallowed convulsively, telling herself she should deny it, even though it was the truth. She didn't want the complication of desiring her husband.

But she'd never stopped desiring him, had she? Sometimes, when the world was asleep and she was alone with her thoughts, she wondered if she still loved him. But that idea was too scary to contemplate.

All she knew now was that she didn't have the strength to walk away from him again. Not when he looked at her with such yearning. Not when her whole body was clamouring for more of the magic only he could provide.

'Gina.' It was a benediction and a plea, maybe even a curse, for Massimo looked like he was in pain. Then his hands closed round her hips, tugging her hard against his crotch.

Her eyelids flickered as she felt the wondrous sensation of his long, hot erection against her core and her abdomen. His solid thighs surrounded her. Everything conspired to remind her of the delicious differences between them. Even fully dressed the contact was incredibly arousing. Liquid heat poured through her, pooling low in her body.

Gina's knees sagged and she anchored her hands on his shoulders, feeling the springy muscle sheathing hard bone. So familiar even after all this time.

Her eyes popped wide when she felt one large hand gather up the fabric of her skirt till, with a waft of cool air, he planted his palm across her thigh, branding her through the fine stocking.

Massimo held her gaze as he slid his palm higher, so high it reached the bare flesh at the top of her stay-up stocking. His touch sent a shock of heat through her, making her unsteady legs wobble harder.

Instantly Massimo coiled his other arm low around her back. But Gina barely noticed. Her attention was focused on his hand as it crested the top of her thigh and slid, centimetre by heart-stopping centimetre, across to the silk covering her femininity.

She couldn't help it. A shudder racked her as long fingers cupped wet silk, moulding to her shape, curling in so that, despite herself, Gina tilted her pelvis up into his touch.

Massimo smiled then. Not a triumphant sneer of victory but an expression of relief. Of thanksgiving.

'Massimo?' The way he looked...

'I couldn't bear to think you didn't want me anymore.' The words were slurred, tripping over each other. But still they imprinted themselves on her brain.

His hand moved and her thoughts scrambled, her eyes slitting against overloading sensation.

It was only when he moved that she roused herself enough to be shocked anew.

Massimo dropped to his knees before her, his left hand raising her dark fuchsia skirt higher and higher till she felt cool air around her pelvis. He splayed his hand over her belly, pinning the bunched fabric there.

Gina looked down on Massimo's thick dark hair, watching it spill over his brow as he moved in and nuzzled her.

The shiver that ripped through her was delight and surprise with a huge dollop of relief thrown in.

How she'd craved his touch. Craved the intimacy of him, the only man she'd ever allowed close. Her heart swelled even as her body softened in surrender and she couldn't find the strength to care.

Gina clamped his shoulders as he tugged at her knickers. She heard a soft curse under his breath, felt the exhalation of warm air on her flesh and heard tearing. Then indigo lace and silk fell to the floor.

Every sense receptor in her body screamed into overdrive as Massimo leaned in again. This time there was absolutely nothing between them. She shuddered at the sensation of his kiss, his lips warm and soft. Then his tongue, sliding down through secret folds, to lap at the tiny bud where pleasure centred.

'Massimo!' Did she cry it out loud? Or was her throat too dry to produce sound? She couldn't hear over the rush of blood pounding in her ears.

She felt his hand slide round to her bare cheeks, urging her forward. Then the thrust of his tongue exactly where she most needed him.

Her knees buckled and Massimo's steely arm wrapped round her thighs, holding her up as she bent over him, hair swinging into her eyes. What she saw, Massimo pleasuring her with his mouth, sent a shower of incendiary sparks shearing through her. Her skin burnt as pinpricks exploded across her flesh. But it was the fiery knot of ecstasy building at her core that undid her.

Each caress ripped another defensive layer free. And when he looked up, eyes locking with hers as he sucked hard, the knot that held her together burst undone. Ribbons of rapture unfurled through her, making her quake from her soles to her eyelashes.

Gina screamed. A shout of ecstasy that might have been his name. All she could comprehend was this man and the crisis that splintered her into fragments then welded her together again into a whole that was shinier, better, more perfect than she'd ever been.

Gina's eyes shut, her body caved and she was lost, utterly, to the moment. Not just the physical release, but the gift that was Massimo, the man she'd adored, doing this to her.

Dimly she wondered that she hadn't collapsed to the floor, despite his supportive hold. It wasn't till sometime later that she realised the floating sensation wasn't just the aftermath of her orgasm, but because Massimo had scooped her into his arms. Heat branded her side as powerful arms cradled her. She felt the racing beat of his heart beneath her ear and inhaled the fresh scent of mountain forests.

Nothing had ever seemed so perfect in her life.

Until she sank onto a bed and opened her eyes to see Massimo fumbling with his clothes, tearing his shirt off and thrusting down his trousers. She heard something rip then he was naked above her, his knees straddling her thighs.

Seven years had changed him. He was still tall and lean but his chest was heavier, his thighs and biceps bulkier. Between his thighs his erection jutted towards her and despite her satiation, Gina felt another squiggle of excitement down low in her pelvis. She'd remembered him as well-endowed. But the sight of him naked and ready told her reality was far superior to memory.

'Lean over.' His voice was gruff but his hands were gentle as he lifted her shoulder and slid the zip of her dress down between her shoulder blades. Then he flicked her bra open.

Gina wriggled, helping him tug the beautiful dress down her shoulders and off her arms. But instead of dragging it all the way off her body, Massimo instead whipped off her silky bra and tossed it over his shoulder.

If she'd had any doubts about what they did, his expression would have changed her mind. Nothing could hide the glitter of sexual excitement, the intense masculine arousal, but she'd swear she saw something like reverence too. And when his hands closed over her breasts, cupping and kneading, she realised his fingers were unsteady.

'You don't know how long I've wanted this.' His words feathered her nipple just before he took it in his mouth and suckled.

Instantly Gina arched high off the bed, one hand grabbing the bedspread, the other fastening in the thick hair on the back of his skull. Between her legs the restlessness became an ache that throbbed incessantly.

Then Massimo was there, the weight of his erection settling between her legs as he braced himself over her.

Green-grey eyes met hers and fire sizzled down her backbone. He opened his mouth as if to speak but when Gina shifted against him, trying to ease the ache of need, his mouth snapped shut and his jaw turned to granite.

Then it was as she remembered, the easy slide, the stretch, the tickle of hairy thighs pushing hers wide, the wondrous sense of oneness. The slow retreat then the hard surge back, pushing her up the bed. The weight of Massimo's gaze pinioning her as effectively as his sexy body. Another thrust and the ripples started, growing and cresting as he huffed a choked breath. Then suddenly it was upon them, breaking over them, tugging them down into a whirlpool of darkness and flaming stars and pleasure so profound it must mark her forever.

They clung together, panting, bodies arching and thrusting, Massimo's mouth at her neck, biting down at that sensitive spot he knew drove her crazy.

Gina opened her mouth to scream but his lips closed on hers, tongue delving deep to mimic the way their bodies mated. Together they rode the storm, huddled close, needing each other as the world turned inside out.

And when it was over, still they clung, bodies entwined, breathing mingled, hearts beating in rhythm.

Gina kept her eyes closed. All she could do was take this one breath at a time. Because the alternative, thinking about what they'd just done, would terrify her.

Because this wasn't over. *They* weren't over.

Spectacular sex was hard to resist. But it was worse than that. Despite what she'd told herself for so long, this wasn't just about physical cravings.

How was she supposed to walk away at the end of the week and take up her life again when everything had changed? No, not changed. She'd just been forced to face the truth she'd avoided for years.

She was still in love with her husband.

Chapter Ten

MASSIMO DIDN'T WANT TO MOVE. He couldn't anyway. He wasn't sure he had the strength to stand.

He and Gina had been voracious for each other. Even in the intervals when, as now, they weren't actually making love, they lay tangled together, bodies entwined as if they couldn't bear to be apart.

Seven years' separation had been incinerated by a passion so consuming Massimo had never known anything like it. He'd lost count of the number of times he'd come. One thing he did know, he was addicted to the sound of Gina's throaty purrs and the hoarse way she called his name as ecstasy took her.

Every time she cried his name it battered home the knowledge that she was his. Finally.

Massimo grinned, his lips curving close to her nipple. He moved his head a little and kissed her there softly. She sighed, moving in her sleep, and tenderness wrapped around him. He'd missed this. Not just the sex, but the intimacy of being together. He wanted—

His stomach gave a loud growl. Then another, reminding him he'd been too busy to eat since breakfast, caught up in the madness that had made today's show such a success.

He glanced over at the digital clock and amended that. Yesterday's show. It was already two in the morning and he had another frantically busy day ahead.

Another loud rumble. Loud enough to wake Gina if it kept up.

Massimo rolled away, frowning. But willpower wouldn't fill his stomach. Reluctantly he got up, padding down the hallway to the kitchen.

A short time later, busy laying out an antipasto platter to take to bed and share with Gina, he sensed something. A change in the atmosphere. His skin tingled as if from an electrical charge. His gaze snapped up.

Instantly his mouth dried as desire punched hard. Every muscle tensed. It was one thing to wander around his apartment naked in the early hours. It was another when Gina did it.

His gaze skated from tousled, bright copper waves to a symphony of pale skin and seductive curves that heated his blood to searing point in a second. His wife wasn't a big woman. She was fine-boned. But every centimetre was packed with delectable curves and intriguing hollows. And the fiery glow of red-gold hair at the apex of her thighs was a beacon, inviting further investigation.

His response was immediate and full-bodied, his erection rising insistently as if he were a randy seventeen-year-old instead of a responsible man of thirty-two.

The fork he'd used to lay out prosciutto and semi dried tomatoes clattered to the island bench. Massimo flexed his fingers. They felt stiff and unwieldy.

His gaze lifted to Gina's smoky eyes. He saw something there that made his pulse hurry and his breath quicken. Not simply physical desire but an expression that made his heart swell with hope. It reminded him that sex wasn't enough. He wanted Gina, not just for tonight. He wanted his wife back. He needed to find a way to rebuild what they'd lost.

'Did you miss me?' His voice was rough, scoured from somewhere deep inside.

Gina smiled, a hint of a dimple showing in one cheek as she sauntered towards him. The smile grew as she rounded the large island bench and saw his massive erection.

Her laughter was a peal of bells on a spring day, the moment of sheer delight when you cleared the ground on a downhill ski run and soared, weightless through the air.

'I did.' She sidled closer and snaffled some cheese off the platter, popping it into her mouth. Her lips were a plush, dark pink from being kissed. Her eyes sparkled like the twilight sky when the first stars came out.

He leaned down and buried his face in the curve of her neck, inhaling the mingled aromas of vanilla, sweet woman and sex.

He'd even missed her unique scent, he realised abruptly.

Massimo's hands closed on her upper arms, holding her just where she was while he lavished open-mouthed kisses across her collar-bone then up her neck.

Urgency engulfed him. This, Gina, them together, felt so right. He needed to hang onto it. Ensure she didn't walk out on him again.

He pulled back, ignoring the screaming protest of his hyper-aroused body. 'It's time we talked, Gina. We have things to discuss.'

She said nothing at first. Then she shifted closer.

'Later,' she purred. Her voice was pure seduction but, he realised, her eyes had lost that slumberous quality. They were bright with—

Massimo's thoughts frayed as her hand closed around his erection, sliding experimentally from base to tip and back again.

He locked his knees, his buttocks bunching as pure longing branded through skin, sinew and muscle. Massimo's eyes closed as Gina folded both hands around his length and squeezed.

He groaned, a shudder ripping from his groin up his spine and down his legs to weld his bare feet to the floor.

Instinctively his hands found her hips, perfect curves and the warm silk of supple flesh.

His woman. His Gina.

His eyes snapped open and his brain cells started to scurry into action.

'Gina, I...'

That dimple danced again in her cheek as she leaned in and let her rosy nipples sway across his torso.

She shifted, moving to kneel before him, except Massimo knew one touch of her mouth would have him detonating. He wanted to make this last. He grabbed her under the arms and lifted her off her feet, watching her eyes widen and her mouth form an O of surprise.

Heat smacked him as he watched her lips.

He had to be crazy, denying himself. But as he lifted her onto a clear space on the wide marble counter, he felt nothing but anticipation and satisfaction at the picture she made, all milk-white skin and burnished, silken hair. Softness and beckoning invitation.

Gina wriggled right to the edge of the counter and spread her knees wide in invitation.

Dimly Massimo thought of the conversation he'd planned to have with her. The understanding they had to reach, the past issues they must discuss. But it could wait. His need, and Gina's, were too pressing right now.

See, she was impatient with even this small delay. She grabbed his hand and licked across his palm, right down to his wrist then slowly back again, finally taking his finger in her mouth and sucking so hard her cheeks hollowed.

His erection jerked in response and a flurry of pinpricks scattered across his upper back and chest while his groin tightened impossibly.

Gina dragged his finger from her mouth with an audible pop. Her lips glistened as she looked up at him, her expression sultry. 'I want you *now*, Massimo.'

He was only too willing to oblige. Which was how he came to ravish his wife on the marble kitchen worktop. After which they were both too exhausted to do more than tumble back into bed and hold each other close.

They never did get around to having that important discussion.

Chapter Eleven

FRUSTRATION WARRED WITH PRIDE, DELIGHT and anticipation as Massimo wrapped his arm around Gina's slender waist and ushered her into the party.

Frustration because, after sleeping late, he'd had to race out of the apartment before Gina woke. Milan meant business and as a CEO Massimo couldn't afford to slack off just for pleasure. Not when he'd invested seven years of his life, plus, he recognised with a pang, his marriage, to drag the company to this point of success.

So he and Gina hadn't talked, not properly. He'd worked all day and by the time he returned she was out doing interviews for her latest film.

What little time they'd had in the apartment had been spent tumbled on Gina's bed, driving themselves to a pinnacle of passion that by rights should have prevented them moving afterwards.

No wonder he smiled broadly as he introduced Gina to the great and the good who'd turned out for tonight's gala. Great sex made even tedious socialising bearable, especially with Gina snuggled up against him, looking like a goddess in that stunning dress of shimmering gold. Later, after he'd ripped it off her, he'd have to find out who designed it. The House of Conti was always looking for new talent.

He caught Gina's eye and saw his own awareness reflected in her glowing look. Satisfaction filled him, and the anticipation of spending the night making love to his gorgeous wife.

Yet he wanted more. Gina had stopped running from him. She touched him all the time, as if, like he, she was powerless to resist the attraction burning so bright between them.

But Massimo didn't merely want a sexy lover. He wanted Gina. The whole package. The woman who'd fascinated him from the first. The woman he'd loved. The woman he'd believed had loved him back...until she walked out on their marriage when he needed her most.

Someone buffeted them from behind and he clamped his hand onto her hip, pulling her close. Her slender form shaped perfectly against him. He splayed his fingers possessively, eliciting a smoky glance full of promise. Fire roared through his veins.

Who knows? After last night she might even be pregnant with his child. For the first time ever he'd been too out of control to take precautions, plus he'd assumed she was protected. It had come as a shock when she'd admitted she wasn't using birth control. That she, like he, hadn't been with anyone else during their separation.

Discovering that had sent a confused tumble of emotions through him. Paramount among them had been gratitude. Because surely it meant she cared, that their marriage still meant something to her.

Her face had flushed when she'd told him. Almost as if she'd been embarrassed to admit it. Her gaze had collided with his, fierce and proud and just a little unsure. In retrospect, he should have recognised she was as uncertain about their relationship as he was, and seized the opportunity to talk. Instead, the news Gina had never been with anyone but him had ignited such a surge of possessive triumph that Massimo had let his libido do the thinking, and seduced her all over again.

Massimo shifted his gaze from the film fan who was talking eagerly to Gina. He wondered if, despite the networking he needed to do tonight, he could get away early and have that heart to heart with Gina. The sooner they established an understanding the sooner—

His thoughts splintered as he looked across the room and saw a tall, older woman, svelte and elegant in a black dress and minimal yet stylish jewellery.

She turned and caught his stare. Even from this distance he read a query in the lift of one eyebrow and in her grey-green eyes. Then she turned to speak to someone and disappeared into the crowd.

What the hell was his mother doing here? Last he heard she was at home looking after his father as she recovered from a winter flu.

Gina made her way back from the ladies room, head pounding and nerves on edge. It wasn't the strangers at the party who bothered her. It was Massimo.

No, that wasn't right. It was herself.

Ever since last night when Massimo had seduced her, and she'd been weak enough to let him, she felt as if she inhabited some fantasy world far removed from reality.

He'd all but dared her to have sex with him and had she resisted? No, she'd melted in a puddle of lust and let him do whatever he wanted with her.

The tragic thing was she'd wanted everything he did to her. And more besides.

Heat crawled up her throat as she remembered how she'd leapt on him as soon as he'd walked in the door this evening. And last night, she'd sashayed naked into the kitchen because when she'd woken alone, fear and loneliness had snaked through her, destroying the fragile Eden they'd created together. She'd had to follow him.

That fear had been reinforced when Massimo wanted to talk. He'd looked so serious she'd panicked, shying from the prospect and deliberately distracting him with sex. Since the febrile glitter in his eyes was purely carnal, she'd guessed he wanted to extend their affair.

Even in her desperate state she knew that would be dangerous. Staying with him longer only fed the hope that this time things could be different. That Massimo wanted the *real* Gina, not some modified version who'd come up to his exacting standards.

When Massimo had revealed he hadn't been with any other woman since her, he'd yanked at her heart. It felt like he'd dragged it from her body, till it lay beating helplessly at his feet. She was so *vulnerable* to that man!

She'd wanted to see his celibacy as proof he cared for her. But if he cared, why be so awful to her in Venice? Why treat her that way? Physically it felt as if she touched heaven when she was with him, but emotionally... Did she dare lay herself open to even more pain than she'd already endured? Did she dare stay with him in the hope that he'd changed?

Gina was torn between hope and fear. The trouble was that life, and Massimo, had taught her to be a realist.

She'd told herself for so long that Massimo was selfish and unsupportive. That she was well rid of him. Yet he only had to crook his finger and here she was, playing the masquerade he'd devised, and worse, stripping herself bare.

It might be just sex for him, but Gina understood with a certainty that lay like a dead cold hand across her heart, that she'd crossed a dangerous boundary. When she gave herself to Massimo she gave everything. Her body but also her heart, her mind, her whole being. She feared when this was over, she'd shatter as she had seven years before, only this time she wouldn't be able to glue the pieces together again.

Because she still loved her husband.

What was she going to do?

'Signorina Moretti?'

Gina looked up to see a handsome older woman step away from the shadows of the anteroom that separated them from the party. There was something familiar about her features. Her eyes were the same colour as—

Gina swallowed hard, recognising the family

resemblance.

'Allow me to introduce myself. I'm Giulia Conti, Massimo's mother.'

The woman who'd abused her over the phone all those years ago. Gina's stomach cramped and her chin lifted defensively. Massimo's family hadn't approved of her and no doubt they didn't like seeing him hooking up with her again – an illegitimate actress whose family tree was hardly illustrious. Was she here to warn Gina off?

'Signora Conti.' Gina inclined her head stiffly.

'Could we go somewhere more private? I need to talk with you.' The older woman looked over her shoulder towards the open doorway to where the party was in full swing. The movement emphasised her patrician profile and the exquisite cut of her smoothly styled hair.

Everything about her spoke of money and refinement. Even her nose seemed designed to look down on lesser beings.

'I'm happy to talk here.' Gina stood straighter, bracing herself for the worst. Surely the woman wouldn't berate her here, though she'd probably hand out a warning about not getting too comfortable with Massimo.

Gina's stomach lurched. As if she could do that! She was living a brief fantasy and she knew it. She hadn't been able to resist the blaze of desire and had finally surrendered to it in the vain hope it would burn itself out.

'Very well.' Giulia Conti lifted her chin and firmed her lips. But instead of appearing disapproving, Gina was intrigued to discover the woman looked nervous. What had she to be nervous about?

'You and Massimo look...happy together.'

Gina didn't respond. What could she say? That they were deeply in lust? *Not* the thing to share with his mother.

The older woman shook her head and sighed. 'I knew this wasn't going to be easy.'

Gina watched curiously, finally taking in Giulia's death grip on her evening purse and the way she kept swallowing as if her throat were dry.

Gina stifled a sigh. 'What can I do for you, Signora Conti?'

Might as well get this over with. She just hoped it wasn't going to be too poisonous.

'I...I'm so pleased to see you and Massimo together.' The woman's grey-green gaze, so like her son's, stopped darting around the small room and fixed on Gina with an intensity that rocked her back on her feet.

'Pardon?'

Giulia's mouth turned down. 'Of course you're surprised.' She paused, swallowing yet again. 'I'm afraid I don't precisely remember everything I said to you all those years ago, but what I do recall is enough to mortify me.'

Gina opened her mouth then shut it, unable to think of anything to say.

The other woman waved one elegantly tapered hand in an abrupt, jerky motion. 'I must apologise for that. Later on, when I realised...' She lifted her shoulders. 'I'd thought I'd have a chance to say sorry in person when you joined Massimo but I never got the opportunity.'

Strangely, Gina didn't hear the censure she'd expected over the fact she hadn't gone to Massimo to live in his family home. What was going on?

'So I'm taking the opportunity now.' The woman's narrow jaw rose and once more she met Gina's bemused stare. 'I don't know how much Massimo has told you about what happened at that time.'

'He said your husband was ill and you needed him there.'

'That's all?' Giulia's eyes narrowed and slowly she nodded. 'I did, desperately. That day you rang I'm afraid I was rather hysterical. To be blunt I was having a complete meltdown. I'd just discovered... things about my husband, about our situation, that rocked me to the core. My world had turned on its head. It was no excuse for the way I reacted to your call and I apologise. You must have thought me a complete harpy.'

Gina had, but seeing the older woman's trembling sincerity, her sympathy rose. There was no doubt this woman was genuinely remorseful.

'Thank you, Signora Conti. I appreciate that.'

Giulia's mouth turned up in a wry smile. 'Signora Conti. That's both of us, even if it's not publicly known.'

Gina's eyes widened. She kept thinking in terms of Massimo's family, Massimo's mother. It was strange to think of this earnest woman as her mother-in-law.

As if she'd read her mind Giulia continued. 'When I heard you and Massimo were together here, I had to see you.'

Here it comes. The sting in the tail.

Gina lifted a hand to brush her hair back off her face in an attempt to appear insouciant. She suspected it didn't work.

Cool, bony fingers closed around her hand as she lowered it, eliciting a ripple of surprise. 'I know it's years late but I wanted to welcome you to the family, my dear. I hope you can forgive me for the things I said to you. They truly weren't about you but about...other matters.'

Gina felt her eyes round. 'They weren't?' she finally managed to whisper.

'No. Though to my shame I'm sure it sounded like it. The truth is I've relied on Massimo far too much, we all have. And supporting us has taken its toll. He deserves happiness. When I saw you both tonight, how happy you are together, it just proved you're the woman for him.'

'Please, Signora Conti.' Gina's head was reeling. It felt like the floor rippled beneath her feet as the world tilted out of alignment. 'You don't understand—'

'Mother!' The word was whiplash sharp, flicking around them. Giulia stiffened, her hold tightening on Gina's fingers.

'Massimo. I was just making Gina's acquaintance.'

Gina turned to see Massimo scowling at them. Obviously he wasn't happy to see her and his mother together.

Because he doesn't want anyone making the mistake of thinking you're a permanent part of his life?

After all, he'd specified he wanted her for a single week. That was all he needed to use her name for his company. And her body for his pleasure.

For some bizarre reason Massimo hadn't taken another lover but it seemed for him that was all they shared – a phenomenal sexual attraction. He hadn't spoken of love, just of want, even in the throes of passion. Maybe he hoped this week would cure him of that? The idea shredded her fragile hopes.

If he'd loved her and aimed to re-establish their marriage he'd have told her in Venice. He wouldn't have been so brutal, forcing her here as his hostess, his pretend partner.

Or, the idea emerged out of nowhere, was this masquerade some sort of twisted payback? Because she hadn't been an obedient wife all those years before?

Suddenly the shock that had held her immobile smashed and hurt poured through the cracks. Gina stepped back on unsteady legs, away from both Contis.

She couldn't think here. She needed to be alone to grapple with her fears and work out what to do.

'Gina, are you all right? You look pale.' The concern in his voice might have been convincing if Gina hadn't spied the gossip columnist who'd appeared in the doorway behind him, her gaze going avidly from one to the other.

Damage limitation. That's what Massimo was doing. He must know they were being watched.

Gina was sick of the pretence. Sick of everything.

She pasted on a stiff smile. 'It was a pleasure to meet you, Signora Conti. But I'm afraid I have to leave. I have quite a headache.'

'I'll take you.' Massimo stepped forward and the pain piercing Gina's chest turned into an ache that spread through her whole body.

'No. Stay and chat with your mother. You still have a lot of people you need to see. I'll catch a taxi.' With that she turned and hurried away.

The glittering crowd was a blur as she stumbled

through it. People called her name and once or twice she caught the flash of a camera but she kept going.

Finally, at the entrance to the grand old building she managed to breathe again. Soon she'd be alone. Soon she wouldn't have to pretend she was all right. Then perhaps she'd be able to wrap her head around what had just happened.

One more step forward and Gina was looking through the glass doors for a taxi when a hand closed hard and hot around her elbow.

Gina didn't turn. She knew Massimo's touch, his presence, his fresh outdoorsy male scent.

A quiver ran through her. She could pretend all she wanted but in reality she was tied to this man by more than sex or his sordid blackmail deal. A silly part of her had thrilled to hear his mother welcome her to the family.

As if there was any chance they could mend their marriage! What they'd shared for those few brief months had been a sweet, heady illusion. They couldn't go back.

'Come, *tesoro*. I'll see you home.'

Gina didn't have the energy to respond but her mouth curved in a crooked smile. Home was the one place she suspected he'd never take her.

Chapter Twelve

IT DIDN'T TAKE LONG TO get back to the apartment. Fortunately Massimo didn't press her to talk on the way. She felt utterly exhausted and not from lack of sleep. Gina was weary with a marrow-deep exhaustion that was emotional, not physical. Every bone and sinew ached with the effort of keeping her head up, her expression bland.

It had been a mistake giving in to Massimo and coming to Milan. It was a mistake spending any time with him at all, as it only made her aware of how invested she still was in him.

But they couldn't continue like this. The time had come for a reckoning. Silently she preceded him into the apartment and made straight for the kitchen. She was turning on the coffee machine when his deep voice wound around her like a physical caress.

'I can do that.'

Gina shook her head. She needed to be busy. Preferably not watching him.

'Gina. Look at me. Please.' There it was again, that hint of desperation that had made a fool of her before. She told herself she wouldn't be taken in by it again. Yet she hesitated.

She felt his tall frame at her back and despite her reservations felt her body tingle, anticipating his touch.

It didn't come. He simply stood, waiting.

Gina huffed out a sigh. Since when had Massimo made anything easy? Except sex of course.

'Very well.' Still avoiding his eyes, she swished her long skirt aside and hoisted herself up onto one of the stools at the granite countertop, resting her feet on the foot bar.

But he made no move to make coffee. Instead he took the stool beside her, spinning hers around till they were facing. He widened his legs so they wrapped either side of hers, heat and muscle imprisoning her. Their eyes locked.

Immediately Gina felt claustrophobic. Panic fluttered high in her throat and she looked away.

'Are you all right? Talk to me, Gina.'

The hoarse note in Massimo's deep voice took her by surprise. As did his question. She'd expected him to ask about what had passed with his mother.

'I'm okay.' Time to draw on her acting skills, for pride's sake.

'Liar.'

The single word jerked her head up.

'Of course you're not okay. I can see that. But whatever the problem is we can deal with it.'

'We can?' Again, not what she expected. 'What exactly do you intend to do?'

'Whatever it takes to make you feel better.' He shrugged, those broad shoulders hemming her in. Except this time she didn't feel claustrophobic.

She felt...protected. Maybe because he'd taken her chilled hands, gently rubbing warmth and comfort into them with his strong thumbs.

'I can look after myself, Massimo. I fight my own battles.' Except at the moment it was herself she fought – the confused self who wanted to surrender everything to this man.

'I don't doubt it. You're a marvellously strong person. You wouldn't have got where you have if you weren't. But wouldn't it be easier to have someone at your side, helping you face any troubles?'

The idea was tempting, so exactly what she'd believed she'd signed up for when they'd married, that for a second Gina was silent. Then she remembered. 'Don't you mean someone who can tell me what to do? Someone to direct my life?'

He sighed and his fingers tightened on hers. Then he let them go, sitting back and running his hand through his hair, pushing it back off his brow.

Strange how his withdrawal hurt, even though it was expected.

'I'm sorry, Gina. I—'

'You already apologised.'

'Not for this. I'm sorry for bringing you into a situation that's quenched all the brightness out of you. I thought I was doing the right thing...' He shook his head. 'I should never have forced you to come here, not without explaining. I'd thought after last night I could make you happy again.'

He looked so grim that to her surprise her wretched heart tugged. Where was her anger? Her disappointment? She was so mixed up.

'You did make me happy. You're a marvellous lover.'

'Is that all?' His eyes captured hers and Gina stared back, not quite believing what she saw.

'Massimo? What are you saying?'

'What I should have said in Venice.' His mouth flattened. 'No, what I should have said years ago except I was too proud and stupid and scared. That life without you isn't any life at all. I love you, Gina. I want you back.'

Shock slammed her back so fast she almost slid off her perch, till Massimo's large hands steadied her. But instead of keeping hold of her, he withdrew his touch as soon as she was steady. As if giving her space to think. Yet not too much space. His long thighs still surrounded hers.

'You love me?'

His mouth settled in a crooked line that hinted at both humour and pain. 'Go on, say it. I've got a strange way of showing it.'

A furtive spark of hope ran like fire through her middle. 'Except in bed.'

The crooked line of his mouth became a lopsided smile. 'That's one thing between us that never changed, did it?'

She felt an answering smile, tight and wry, curl her lips, even though her brain was a whirling mess of contradictory ideas.

'I hate seeing you upset, Gina. I want to put things right so you'll be happy.'

Gina shook her head, wonderingly. 'Maybe they can't be put right.'

'I'd still like to be with you, trying. I know life has ups and downs. We can't always be happy. But I want us to be together. I want to be your husband, properly this time. For the rest of our lives.'

A gasp gathered in her mouth and her eyes widened. 'Then why were you so cruel in Venice? So... judgemental?' The recollection of his words had haunted her since.

'Jealousy. Frustration. Pride. Hurt. You name it.'

Gina blinked up at him but for once Massimo's expression was unguarded. It was like browsing an open book and what she saw there made her heart catch.

'You mean it!' She felt dazed, wobbly with shock.

'Of course I mean it.' He grabbed her hands. 'It took me a while to realise, though. I spent too long being offended that you didn't see things the way I did. But I never stopped loving you.'

'I'd never have guessed.' It wasn't meant as a barb, but it spurred him on.

'I know. I was callow for all I thought myself so mature. I made a mess of everything.'

Gina thought of what his mother had said, about some terrible revelation affecting his family and her having a complete meltdown. Clearly things had been worse with his family that she'd imagined.

'It was a difficult time. Your father needed you.' She hesitated, then pushed out the words that had haunted her conscience for seven years. 'I was jealous myself, of your family. They called and you went straight to them, without taking me. You'd think I'd have been more understanding. I'd always wanted a close family.'

Instead her mother had never been particularly maternal and Gina didn't know her father. She'd wanted, more than anything, to belong, but when Massimo put his family first in a time of crisis, instead of supporting him, she'd taken offence, believing it proved he didn't really love her.

Massimo squeezed her hands.

'You wouldn't have wanted mine, at least not then. They were a mess. In the beginning I didn't take you with me because I didn't want you to see them at their worst. I thought it would be too overwhelming. It was just as well you didn't accept my ultimatum later to give up your career to live with me in the family home.' He shook his head. 'It was stupid of me but in my defence I was desperate.'

'You were? You always seemed so much in control.' Had that been a front?

His laugh was bitter. 'That's a joke. I was out of my depth but determined not to go under.'

'Tell me, Massimo.' Years ago she'd asked him to explain why it was so vital he give up his career and stay with the family. He'd refused. Would he now?

Slowly he nodded. 'I went home because of my father's heart attack. But when I arrived I discovered there was much more. It's not pretty.'

Gina said nothing, just waited.

'It turns out the heart attack happened while he was having sex. With his secretary.'

She couldn't stop the gasp that escaped. 'I had no idea.'

'Not many did. It was hushed up. Apparently the affair had been going on for quite some time. He'd deluded himself into thinking she cared for him rather than his money. He'd been spending lavishly, luxury *business* trips away, jewellery. He even bought her an apartment. He was so besotted he stopped taking an interest in the business and spent his time filching from it to buy more and more extravagant treats.'

Massimo paused and rolled his shoulders as if relieving stiffness there. 'Not only was the old man fighting for his life, we discovered he'd all but bankrupted the business that four generations of my family had built. The business that was to provide for my younger siblings and support my parents in old age. They were on the cusp of losing everything, including the house. On top of that my mother had a breakdown. She loved him, you see. She had no idea of his double life.'

Gina curled her fingers around Massimo's, remembering his mother's sense of guilt and her determination to apologise. 'Your poor mother.'

'It was tough on her. But she's come through it all okay.' His mouth tugged up grimly at one side. 'She even forgave him, eventually. She nursed him back to health, though he never fully recovered. He's a changed man, for the better, despite his health issues.'

'No wonder they needed you.'

Massimo lifted his shoulders. 'There was no-one else in the family able to take control. Plus it turned out that the two most trusted managers in the company had taken advantage of my father's distraction to dip their fingers in the till too. The company was on the brink of going under.'

Gina leaned towards him. 'Why didn't you *tell* me, Massimo?'

'Because I was young and stupid. You hadn't even met my family and I was wary about airing all that dirty laundry straight away. I suppose I was ashamed. I wanted to fix things before you knew the worst but it turned out that took years.' His mouth flattened. 'It would have been easier if I'd already told them about you, but they'd had such set ideas about who I should marry, it seemed better to give them a fait accompli. Except when I got there they weren't up to any more surprises. Stupid of me. They'd have coped. They only had to meet you to know what a treasure you are.'

'And then I refused to join you.' Gina felt ancient guilt cut her down to size.

'In retrospect I can't blame you. I'd taken it for granted you'd drop everything to be with me. When you didn't I got scared, especially when I recalled how my father had lied to my mother and abused her trust—'

'You thought I'd been unfaithful?' Horror filled her.

'No. But my ego was such I thought you'd just do what I wanted, no matter the consequences. That's when I started demanding, not asking. I realised later it was unreasonable to expect you to walk out on your first major movie role. But at the time I couldn't see straight.'

'Oh, Massimo. I wish I'd known. I feel dreadful. I was so worried about not becoming a doormat, and I was scared of your family too.' She swallowed hard, tasting misery on her tongue. 'I should have gone to you, even if it was only to argue things through. But I was scared. I worried maybe they were right and I was inferior wife material. It was cowardly of me.'

His eyebrows climbed his forehead. 'You, inferior? Never in a million years.' Massimo shook his head, incredulity clear in his expression. 'My parents were messed up, *cara*, but they're not stupid. They could never think that.'

Gina lifted one shoulder. 'When I realised you hadn't told them about me I thought you were ashamed of me.'

His crack of laughter reverberated around the room. 'Ashamed? You're the most talented, beautiful, wonderful woman I know. I was blessed to have you in my life.' Massimo's expression sobered. 'I just hope I can persuade you to come back to me.'

'That's really what this is about? A reconciliation?' Strange how her voice managed to sound even, despite her breathlessness.

His bright gaze caught hers and clung. 'Is it such a bad idea? I know I've got a lot to learn about being a decent husband. I made so many mistakes—'

Gina pressed a finger to his lips. 'We both made mistakes. I should have trusted you more instead of letting fear get the better of me. I had a chip on my shoulder about not being good enough for the Contis and—'

'Not good enough!' He dragged her hand from his mouth but didn't relinquish his grip on her wrist. 'You're the love of my life, *mio dolce amore.*'

Suddenly she was blinking back tears. 'Oh, Massimo. I love you too. I never stopped caring for you, even when I pretended I didn't. When I think of the time we've wasted...'

'Sh, little one.' He cupped her cheek. 'It's all right. Especially since you love me.' The grin that broke across his face was so brilliant it made her smile through her tears. 'It's exactly what I've wanted to hear, for so long.'

'But all those years...'

Massimo shook his head. 'What's done is done. Besides, I know I for one wasn't as mature as I'd thought when we got married. I had to learn about give and take, and respecting my partner as well as loving her.'

'And I had to learn about trust.'

'And believing in yourself,' he added. He paused and drew a breath so deep his whole chest expanded. 'The question is, do you believe in us? Is there a chance we could start again?'

Gina smiled up into the face of the only man she'd ever loved, her heart bursting with joy. 'We already have, haven't we? And if we take things one step at a time—'

'We won't make the mistakes we did the first time. And when we make other mistakes we'll sort them out *together*.' His deep voice made it sound like a vow. She felt his sincerity in every syllable.

An instant later he was standing before her, bending down to loop his powerful arms about her and lift her into his embrace.

'Massimo? What are you doing?' She was breathless, putting her hands around his neck.

'Taking the first step.'

He turned towards the door and was soon striding down the corridor.

Gina laughed, buoyed by excitement and hope. 'And of course that first step is towards the bedroom.'

Massimo stopped and looked down at her. Gina's heart stuttered at what she read in his face. 'We deserve to celebrate, my love. But believe me, I intend to be with you, no matter where our path leads. We're staying together.'

Gina nodded her agreement. 'Always.'

Massimo bent his head and captured her lips in a tender kiss, carefully sealing that *Always* between them.

Epilogue

'IT'S A TRIUMPH. SUCH A masterful piece of directing. And your performance...' The film critic leaned towards Gina, ensuring she heard him over the noise of the opening night party. 'Just superb.' He kissed his fingers so enthusiastically she grinned.

'She is, isn't she?' Massimo's deep voice, smug with pride, rumbled from beside her and his arm slid more snugly around her waist, pulling her close against him.

Gina thanked the critic then said to her husband, 'He's talking about the *performance*, Massimo.'

Massimo regarded her minutely. 'The performance, yes. And the woman too. Just superb.'

The look he bestowed on her wasn't what you usually saw at red-carpet premieres, surrounded by the cream of Rome's beautiful people. It was something you might, but only if you were extraordinarily lucky, see in private. And only then if you'd found the one person in the world who understood, appreciated and loved you completely.

Gina had found just that.

The knowledge was still wondrous, though she and Massimo had been together since Fashion Week in Milan, over a year ago. It hadn't all been smooth sailing, but they'd learned to talk through differences, to share and listen, and as a result their relationship grew stronger every day.

As she stared up at him, her heart softened, and her knees too, making her grateful for his proprietorial grip.

Dimly she was aware of the critic chuckling, murmuring something more, then excusing himself.

Massimo lifted her hand, brushing his lips over her knuckles. 'My beautiful, talented wife.'

She should take issue with the way he sidetracked her when she was supposed to be talking to people about the movie. But how could she when he made her feel so good? 'What am I going to do with you, Massimo?'

His lips tickled her ear. 'Take me to bed?'

Gina jumped as he nipped her ear lobe and darts of fire shot to every erogenous zone in her body.

'Massimo!' It was Giulia's voice, cultured and clear, that broke their intimacy. 'Haven't I taught you to behave better than that? Stop distracting Gina and let her shine. This is her moment.'

Massimo straightened and Gina saw her mother-in-law had cornered them, discreetly blocking them from the crowd beyond. But despite admonishing her son, Giulia's eyes were bright with amusement. In anyone less refined that flicker of an eyelid might even have been a wink.

'She is shining. Can't you see?' Massimo's tone was light with laughter but there was a depth to his words, a sincerity, that filled Gina with warmth.

'Of course I can. Now, stop being selfish and let her circulate. I see Angela and Matteo De Laurentis just there. Why don't you join them? It would be the perfect photo opportunity to promote the film.'

'And the Conti label,' Massimo murmured. For Roberto, the House designer, had produced a fabulous gown just for Gina. The gossamer-fine fabric was in green shot through with a deep blue that perfectly matched her eyes. The dress clung to her figure before falling in delicate folds to the floor. It left enough bare skin to show off the flawless sapphire pendant Massimo given her and Gina had spied plenty of envious stares.

'It's an honour to have you wearing the label, my dear.' Giulia pressed her fingers round Gina's. 'And a joy to have you in the family.'

'Thank you. That means so much to me.' It still stunned Gina how easily she'd become part of the Conti clan. How much fun Massimo's siblings were and how welcome they'd all made her.

Massimo and Gina were crossing the room towards their friends when Massimo paused, pulling her to a halt. She looked up to see him frowning.

'You *did* want to wear the dress, didn't you?' It was unlike Massimo to sound unsure and his uncertainty tugged at her heart. 'Roberto was so eager to make something special for you but I didn't want you feeling obliged—'

'Sh.' Gina put her finger on his lips. 'We've been through this before. I *adore* the dress. How could I not? It's utterly gorgeous and it was designed especially for me in a colour I love.'

Still Massimo looked serious and Gina was forced to take drastic action. She leaned up on tiptoe and kissed his jaw, then the corner of his mouth, then—

'Gina Conti, stop distracting me! I'm trying to do the decent thing and share you. This is your night. It's time to let you shine.'

'But I *am* shining, Massimo. Can't you see?' She smiled as she mimicked his earlier words. She felt as if she'd swallowed whole galaxies of sparkling stars.

Massimo's gaze darkened and he wrapped his arms around her, oblivious of the crowd and the buzz of conversation.

'Absolutely. You shine brighter than the moon itself. You're the light of my life, Gina.'

'And you're mine, Massimo.'

Then to the delight of friends, family and photographers alike, they forgot the opening night crowd completely.

IF YOU ENJOYED THIS STORY please tell your friends or consider writing a review.

❧

YOU MIGHT ALSO LIKE OTHERS IN THIS SERIES:

HOT ITALIAN NIGHTS ANTHOLOGY,
BOOKS 1-3
Back in the Italian's Bed
Bought by the Italian
Bound to the Italian Boss

HOT ITALIAN NIGHTS ANTHOLOGY,
BOOKS 4-6
The Italian's Bold Reckoning
At the Italian's Bidding
Falling for the Brooding Italian

BOOK EIGHT – Burning for the Italian

❧

For other Annie West titles visit
www.annie-west.com

About Annie

ANNIE WEST LOVES WRITING SEXY, emotional stories about charismatic heroes and strong heroines, and not just because it gives her a chance to ignore housework! She is a USA Today Bestselling author, published in 25 languages, and has won the Romantic Times Reviewers' Choice Award and the Romance Writers of Australia Romantic Book of the Year.

She lives on the east coast of Australia between wonderful beaches and glorious wine country. When not writing and avoiding housework she can be found walking, enjoying good food and good company, travelling or reading. Annie loves chatting with readers as far apart as Brisbane, Bremen and Bermuda.

Visit Annie at *www.annie-west.com*

Sign up for her reader newsletter for advance notice of new releases, giveaways and behind the scenes info via her website.

Or follow her on Facebook at
www.facebook.com/anniewest.author

Printed in Great
Britain
by Amazon